SECRET OF THE BLACK PLANET

By
MILTON LESSER

I0616910

ARMCHAIR FICTION
PO Box 4369, Medford, Oregon   97501-0168

*For more information about Armchair Books and products, visit our
website at…*

www.armchairfiction.com

Or email us at…

armchairfiction@yahoo.com

MYSTERY IN THE ASTEROID BELT

His name was John Hastings…or was it? No…it was Bok-kura, the Jovian Strong Man who thrilled untold thousands in Dufree's circus sideshow. Bok-kura had very big muscles and almost no problems—until a girl from Mars made a remark that got him elected as the man most likely to be murdered!

But he was a man with no past, at least not one he could remember. Then his memories started to come back—slowly. Memories that would eventually lead him to Mars, and soon after, the mysterious Asteroid Belt—within which lay the secret of his past. But even more so, the secrets of Mankind's past, as well as its future. Come along with master sci-fi storyteller Milton Lesser as he spins one of his finest tales.

FOR A COMPLETE SECOND NOVEL, TURN TO PAGE 113

CAST OF CHARACTERS

JOHN HASTINGS

He had discovered a secret that could change the course of all life in the Solar System. If only he could remember what it was!

ELLEN CREWSON

It's tough being an intelligent, beautiful woman—and having the man you love not even remember who you are.

SUUKI

His underground brotherhood wanted to gain control of the secret that all men dream of…eternal life.

DR. ELKINS

This Martian-based doctor was determined to save Hastings' life. As it turned out, his skills weren't needed at all.

PEREZ

At 500 pounds, he was the fattest man you could ever want to know. A circus sideshow was the perfect place for him.

DUFREE

He was the mean-spirited boss of a circus sideshow, but some of his best attractions were more than just the usual circus freaks.

IG KARNJUD

Like most of the inhabitants of Mars, this big Martian didn't know how to swim, but he decided to go rafting anyway.

CHAPTER ONE
Mystery Man

MY NAME? Hell, I don't know. Any name will do, but you might call me John Hastings, for that was what the girl called me just before someone tried to kill me.

One thing for sure—don't go around saying I'm Bok-kura, StrongMan of Jupiter. Sure, I'm strong, damn strong, and I've got reflexes so fast they'd make your hair stand on end, like all the sideshow blurbs say. But don't call me Bok-kura, not unless you want to see that strength and those reflexes go to work on you!

I'd just about decided to give up this StrongMan stuff anyway. I couldn't look at myself in the mirror anymore. You see, you lift weights, no phonies, but legitimate three or four-hundred-pound barbells. You bend iron rods and watch all the girls in the audience gasp. You beat up a few of the local strong boys when the show is on the road. For that you get room and board and a couple of solars spending money each week.

But one question keeps nagging at your brain. It's there every time you stop long enough to think. It's there before you go to sleep at night, your muscles stiff and aching. And it's there when you wake up in the morning, the Fat Man of Venezuela snoring contentedly on the next cot. Most of all, it's there all the while you're performing, the big mirrored walls throwing your reflection back at you and mocking you with it.

Who am I?

Not Bok-kura, not the StrongMan of Jupiter. Oh, they call me that, but it's a lot of hogwash. Don't ask me how I know. I know. One day about two or three years ago, they found me down at the Spaceport knocking some sense into a couple of drunks who thought an off-duty spaceliner hostess was something you played with. They dragged me away so fast that the girl didn't even have time to thank me. I've been Bok-kura the Strong Man ever since.

What about before that day at the Spaceport? Don't look at me like that—I can't remember a thing. Nothing. And so I'm Bok-kura.

The figment of an eager promotion man's interplanetary imagination, with about as much personal identity as a cubic mile of deep space...

IT was a weekday evening, with not much of a crowd out here in the Iowa sticks where space travel is still so much of a novelty that it brings the whole county out to watch every time an old battered circus cruiser comes snorting down on its faltering rockets. After that, most of them go home. They wanted to see the ship, not what was inside it.

When the girl came in, she stopped the show as far as I was concerned. Not for long, only for a moment or two, long enough to take a good look at her. The cheap and gaudy dames of the solar run, with their painted faces and wagging hips, they're all right for a night's entertainment when you feel you need it. So's a bottle of Venusian brandy sometimes, but it doesn't make you think of a little cattle ranch on one of the Jovian moons, with a soft-glowing dome and a picket fence and all the trimmings.

This girl did.

Only I hardly had time to think about it, for she took one look at me sweating with my barbells and her face got all chalky white. She gave a little yelp and she cried, "John Hastings! You're John Hastings!"

Not much, really. But it got a rise out of me. I've kept a little card in my pocket ever since I can remember. Grubby and tattered, it had a few words scrawled on it hastily: *Have caution, John Hastings, they may try to kill you.*

One plus one, together they equal two. And John Hastings plus John Hastings? I didn't know, but maybe the girl could help me find out.

I put the barbell down too fast, and a muscle twinged dangerously in my abdomen. Then I think I jumped off my platform, and the way I came at her must have frightened the girl, for she backed up a quick step or two. "I'm sorry if I startled you," she said, looking at my face. "But I thought—"

"What did you think?" Sometimes I wish I could modulate my voice and sound like a tenor. I was trying to be gentle, but when I'm ruffled, my voice has a way of rumbling up from deep inside my throat, and I guess my attempt at gentleness didn't come off.

"All right," the girl told me curtly, regaining her composure, "you don't have to get angry. I just thought you looked like someone I used to know. It's impossible, of course—"

"Like John Hastings?"

"Yes, like John. That's what I said. You even sound like him, a little. Forget it, Mr. Strong Man. I'm imagining things." She turned on her heel and started to walk from the room.

Dufree came in then, and you don't play around on Dufree's time, not if you want to keep your job. I took one quick step after the girl, but Dufree nodded his suave good looks toward my platform and I hopped back on it. Maybe I'd been taking orders for so long I'd got used to it, I don't know.

Dufree scowled. "Chase after the local gals like that, Bokkura, and I'll have to let you go. If you think I'm joking, go ahead and try it."

I DIDN'T. Instead, I had a better idea. Perez the Fat Man carried five hundred pounds around with him, but once he got started Perez could travel under a pretty good head of steam. And Perez wasn't slated to go on for another hour yet.

He lolled off in an alcove watching me perform and smoking a big cigar, the sweat rolling down his cheeks in little streams, which came together at the rolls of fat under his chin. After Dufree left, I beckoned the Fat Man toward me, and he waddled ponderously forward.

I asked him, "Would you like to add my solars to yours next week?"

"That depends on what I've got to do. It's awful hot, Boky, and I'm awful big."

Bok-kura was bad enough. I kind of saw red when someone called me Boky. But this time I let it pass. "Did you see that girl who just left?"

He gave a long low whistle and wiped the sweat from his cheeks with a damp bandana. "Lord, it's hot out here in the summer. We shoulda been on Mars for the season, Boky. Yeah, I saw her. So what?"

"So this. Follow her and let me know where she goes, and you get my credits. Okay?"

Perez shrugged and the fat jiggled up and down under his chin. "It's awful hot—"

"Two weeks, damn it!"

"And I got a lot of weight to tote around—"

"Three! Get the hell out of here now."

Perez shuffled his feet inside the special shoes that helped support his five hundred pounds. "A month?" he asked me, yawning.

"A month! Okay, but you get nothing if you lose her."

Perez stopped his shuffling, leaned forward and dragged his feet. Inertia helped him and soon his bulk squeezed through the doorway and disappeared.

I felt like laughing. There was a fine quarter-ton shadow to put on someone...

Five minutes later, a man I'd never seen before tried to kill me.

IT HAPPENED like this: three or four people stood around while I got ready to press a three-hundred-pound barbell. Try it with half that weight when you have the chance. It isn't easy, and it requires all the concentration you can muster. But thanks to the girl I felt in no mood to concentrate, and that probably saved my life.

Briefly, I let my eyes wander over the audience, brought the bar up halfway and then started to strain. A nondescript figure of a man stood right up front, reached inside his jumper and came up with what looked like a needle gun. I think it was a needle gun, although I'm not sure. Whatever it was, I had a pretty good hunch it could kill me.

The man pointed it at my chest, and no one saw him do it. They all watched me.

I lunged forward with the three-hundred-pound barbell still poised over my head. When I let it go, people started screaming, including the nondescript man who pointed his needle gun at my chest.

He threw up his hands involuntarily and when the bar struck there was a crunching sound. He started to fall and the weight fell with him, landing with the bar across his chest and the disks barely touching the ground on either side. He couldn't have been pinned better if someone had stuck a spike through his chest. He lay there moaning weakly and no one would have placed a bet regarding the state of his rib case. His arms lay limp, the right one flopping about a little. The needle gun had clattered away on the floor somewhere, into Perez's alcove perhaps.

Someone screamed again, not the nondescript man. Dufree came in, very grim and very angry. He took the situation in at a glance, said: "Was that an accident?"

Maybe this had finally done it. Maybe now I could go around finding out the things I had to know. Or maybe it was only temporary, but I felt pretty cocky then. "Does it look like an accident?" I demanded.

"Don't get snooty, Bok-kura. I asked you a question."

"I heard you. Why don't you find out for yourself?"

"Why don't I—" He turned white, not as white as the girl, but white enough. "First," he said, "you're fired. Second, I'm going to call the police as soon as we can get your bar off this man. Come on, lift it up!"

"You lift it," I suggested. There was an old me somewhere deep inside, and at least for now it had come to the surface. Bok-kura performed his feats docily, like a well-trained animal. But someone else didn't.

John Hastings?

"You know I can't budge that," Dufree protested.

"Get someone to help you on the other side and you can roll it off him."

"Roll it! We'd break his ribs, if they aren't broken already. He could sue."

I muttered something about that being a shame, and then I began to walk out.

"Does someone have a gun!" Dufree cried. "I want to keep him here for the police. Doesn't anyone have a gun? Nothing?" And then he was grunting, and I assumed he had set about trying to move the barbell. For a moment I hoped quite cheerfully that he'd crush every rib in the man's chest, but then I found myself walking back inside.

I grabbed one of the disks and heaved up and over with the bar, placing it down gently on the floor. The man continued to groan as if I hadn't done a thing. At first I wanted to remain and question him, but it looked a lot like his answers would consist only of groaning, for a few hours at least. I turned to walk away again, flung Dufree off when he clung half-heartedly to my arm. Someone stood off in a comer with one of those new wrist phones, dialing the police probably.

The meant it was time for me to do like Perez—to scram, and fast. Perez!

SOMETIMES you can be fourteen different varieties of an idiot. How could I leave without hearing from Perez? The girl with her John Hastings had started this whole thing, and I wouldn't have been too surprised if Perez turned up with a connection between her and the nondescript man with the needle gun.

I ducked around the vacant lot and into the small bunk-room that I shared with the Fat Man, stripped out of my StrongMan getup and donned a jumper and a pair of leatheroid slacks. A moment later I ran out the back way and caught a glimpse of Dufree and another man approaching the front entrance warily. I thought the other man carried a gun, but it could have been my imagination.

A ditch separated the lot from a good two-lane highway, which cut out across the prairie straight as a plumb line toward Cedar Rapids, thirty miles away. I stretched out full-length in the ditch and prepared to wait. It might be long wait at that, for Perez wouldn't exactly fly back with his information—*if* he got any.

A few jetcars streaked by on the highway, zooming off in the direction of Cedar Rapids. The sun hung low on the Western horizon, and off to the South a big thunderhead was piled high, billowing mass atop billowing mass. The whole thing rumbled ominously as it reared its dark head over the flatlands, and an occasional flash of lightning knifed through the sky.

In big lazy drops at first, the rain started to come down. But then the wind kicked up a bit and the thunderhead soared still higher. The wind stopped abruptly, leaving every thing on the prairie as still as the red wastelands of Mars between dust storms.

Then the rains came, sheet after sheet of them. The dry prairie could sop them up so fast that the ground almost didn't get wet. But my ditch couldn't, and I almost thought I'd have to swim away before Perez returned.

BY THE TIME it got dark, a jetcar of police had arrived from Cedar Rapids, and soon I could see them probing through the rain with their search beams. Dimly, I heard Dufree telling them what had happened. It seemed his StrongMan of Jupiter wasn't of Jupiter at all. Just a bum he'd picked up one day at the New York Spaceport a couple of years ago, a bum he'd never trusted, but hell, business was business and anyway he was insured, so could they just issue an alarm and then clear off his lot and let business resume? What…the injured man? Dufree thought he was alive, but he couldn't be sure.

Four policemen had piled out of the jetcar, and now with the midway lights overhead, only three returned to it. One would remain on with the circus, despite every thing Dufree could say about that sort of thing being bad for business.

For once I agreed with Dufree. I didn't like the idea either not while I had to wait for Perez.

He returned not ten minutes after the jetcar roared away. The rain had slowed to a trickle and the air had become hot and sultry again, like it always does so soon after a Midwestern summer storm. I could see the headlights of Perez's obsolete automobile from far off, coming slowly up the highway. The Fat Man couldn't get inside a standard model jetcar, and a special job would be too expensive. He used a rebuilt fifty-year-old auto instead, with the front seat flung all the way back and the shaft of the steering wheel lengthened to extend up over his paunch. I darted out of the ditch and trotted up the road, flagging Perez down a good three hundred yards from the lot. The car clattered to a stop and Perez oozed out through the front door like one big mass of thick syrup.

"Well?" I said.

Perez mopped his soaking brow. "Why couldn't you meet me back at the lot? And where's my solars?"

"You'll get them each week. Think I have them saved up or something?" It was a lie, and I never liked telling lies, but if I told Perez I'd been fired, he might decide to forget about the whole thing. "Now, what did you find out?"

"Well, it wasn't easy. Look, she had one of them jets and I had to follow in this automobile. But Perez is smart, Boky, and don't you forget it. Know what I done?"

I said no, I didn't.

"I checked with the highway police outside of Cedar Rapids. They gotta register every vehicle entering a Spaceport city. I described the gal and they remembered her. Hell, you don't forget a dish like that so easy.

"Anyway, you know where she went?"

Perez took out the stub of a cigar and lit it, puffing furiously and making the sweat come to his cheeks again. "To the Port, that's where." An edge of finality had come to his voice, and he squeezed in again through the doorway of his automobile.

"That's all?" I wanted to know.

"Sure, Boky. That's what you're gonna pay me for, to find out where she went. I found out, so you'll pay."

"Do you know anything else?"

"I ain't saying. A bargain's a bargain." Perez rubbed his short, thick hands together, forgot to wipe away the sweat which was dribbling off his chin. "Lord, I'm hungry."

I reached into my jumper pocket, came up with all the loose change I had. "Here. Now, what else do you know?"

PEREZ'S BEADY little eyes blinked in their folds of fat. "I told you old Perez was a smart cookie. You bet, Boky…"

"What else, damn it!"

"Relax. Just relax. A man's liable to get all hot and bothered in this weather. I went to the Spaceport and found out the gal had a ticket on the Mars liner—"

"Mars!"

"Like I said, Mars."

"What time does it blast off?" I asked the question automatically, but it might as well have been Pluto. You don't earn enough money to book passage on one of the big liners by working in a circus sideshow. Not in a whole year you don't.

"I dunno. But the liner was in its blasting pit, and the pit boys were busy carting their grease cans away from the runners. Pretty soon, I'd say."

I nudged Perez with my elbow until he got the idea and moved his bulk over to the other side of the seat. I climbed in beside him. "You're taking me to Cedar Rapids," I said.

"You're crazy, Boky! I'm overdue already."

"Okay, have it your way. But I got into a fight back at the midway, and I hurt a man. The police are after me, Perez. I hurt one man, and I guess another won't make much difference. Cedar Rapids, Perez?"

He looked at me for a long time, and I couldn't tell what he was thinking because his eyes were hidden in their bags of fat. He started the car and then I heard a scraping noise as he muttered something about those damned gears. He swung the car around in a wide turn and started back toward Cedar Rapids.

I found myself wondering how we'd get past the highway patrol outside Cedar Rapids. I didn't know how, but I felt we could do it. I wasn't Bok-kura any longer, timid for all his strength. I was John Hastings—whoever John Hastings was...

I think Perez must have sensed it.

A SLIVER of a moon had peeped out from among the scattering clouds by the time we reached the highway patrol station. Ahead we could see the lights of Cedar Rapids, a small city suddenly grown big with the coming of space travel. And off to the left the Spaceport itself was a pulsing glow on the horizon.

Perez hadn't uttered a word in the thirty miles of bumpy driving, but now he asked me, "Just how do you intend to pass them, Boky? Tell me that, eh?"

He'd slowed the car to a crawl and now I climbed over the seat and hunkered down behind it. "Listen," I hissed, "you'd better play along." I guess I sounded tough, I don't know. I'd never sounded tough about anything before, not as far as I could recollect, and I think I must have found the new role to my liking.

"Yeah..." from the way he spoke, Perez must have been sneering. "and what if I don't?"

"Well, I didn't do anything that would keep me in jail forever, Perez. Just remember that. When you reach the patrol, you're alone in this contraption, understand?"

Perez muttered to himself, braked the auto to a stop when we neared the patrol gate.

A voice said: "Jeez, where'd you get this car, a museum or something?" Voices always sound more ominous in the darkness, and I was plenty worried. But then the voice took on a touch of laughter. "Oh, it's you, Skinny! You just passed through here a while ago."

" 'Smatter," Perez grumbled, "there a law against it?"

"Nope, just checking. That *is* the law."

"Well, I forgot something in Cedar Rapids, so I'm going back."

"Umm-mm. Guess I don't have to check your credentials again."

"Suit yourself. I got nothing to hide, but I wish you'd lemme drive off and get outa this damned heat!"

"Sure. Okay, go ahead. If you're back before midnight my shift ends then—you can pass right through, Skinny. I'll recognize this thing you travel in. Hah-hah, that's good. Think—"

"I really couldn't say," Perez admitted honestly enough. "I don't know when I'll be back, but I hope it's soon."

By then I'd begun to breathe easily, if quietly, but I was unduly optimistic. The officer hadn't finished yet.

"Say, I remember! You was from that there circus."

"Yeah. I play the skeleton man." Perez's laughter was louder than the officer's.

"What ya think of the guy who went nuts?"

"Who's that?"

"The Strong Man, whatzisname? Bok-kura."

"Search me." Perez shrugged mountainously. "I got back there after it happened. Well, can I go? I'd like to get me a nice cool gin and tonic in town, officer."

"Guess so. Have a sip for me, will ya? S'long, Skinny."

Perez scraped the gears into their low speed once more, and we were on our way. I was grinning when I climbed back over the front seat. "Perez," I chortled, "you were magnificent."

"Yeah? I got me a hunch old Dufree hates your guts after tonight. All right, I wouldn't mind squatting on Dufree and crushing a couple of his scrawny bones. Maybe that's why I'm helping you. Where to, Boky?"

I said the Spaceport and settled back, almost able to enjoy the bouncing ride of Perez's antiquated vehicle. A mile must have passed before I realized he'd called me Boky.

THE GIRL at the information desk smiled professionally. "Yes, sir?"

"When's the next liner taking off for Mars?"

She consulted a chart. "In two months, sir. The fifteenth of September."

"Huh?" I turned to Perez. "I thought you said—"

"Yeah, that's what I said. She got a ticket to Mars. A one-way ticket."

I frowned. "Two months in advance—"

The girl smiled professionally again. "Too bad, if you wanted to get to Mars. You just missed the boat, you know."

I asked her what she meant. "The *Queen* blasted off forty-five minutes ago, sir."

"Oh, I see. Say, can I get a Mars boat someplace else?"

"Yes. Yes, you could do that." She consulted another chart. "White Sands, New Mexico, in five weeks. Or New York in six. Nothing sooner than that. Shall I call for a reservation?"

I shook my head. "No, don't bother."

We got as far as the door to the administration building, Perez beginning to puff and snort. We got no further.

Someone came in and pointed a finger at me. Thin, medium height, nondescript. The man who'd tried to kill me!

Two policemen closed in, their blasters ready. I guess I was struck dumb. I just stood there, my mouth hanging open foolishly. Sure, Dufree could have put two and two together. Perez was missing. I was missing. We roomed together. A cinch. They checked with the highway patrol, found Perez had come this way.

But that wasn't it. Last time I'd seen the nondescript man, he'd been stretched out on the floor, a three-hundred-pound weight across his chest. Probably a few ribs were broken. At the very least, both his arms had been shattered. Now he stood in the doorway with a cold smile on his lips, pointing an accusing finger at me. He didn't exactly look the healthy type, but I'd have bet he was never any healthier than at that moment. Despite enough broken bones to keep him in the hospital for a couple of months.

"...right, friend," one of the policemen was saying, "don't try anything. Just come with us."

The fat quivered on Perez's jowls as he shook his head from side to side. "Not me, officer. You don't mean me too. I ain't got nothing to do with this. I just want a big cool drink."

"It looks a lot like you helped him get away. Come along."

"Helped him!" Perez blubbered. "Not me, sir. Oh no, not me. Why, he forced me. Yes, he forced me. He said, 'Perez, if you—' "

"That's enough! You're coming too."

They came toward us slowly, and I did a lot of quick thinking. Apparently no one knew of the nondescript man's needle gun. No one knew he'd tried to kill me. But they all saw me go wild, all saw the way I'd lunged forward with a three-hundred-pound weight and hurled it at him.

Maybe I could get off with six months or something, I didn't know. But hell, the girl had gone to Mars, with a one-way ticket. And the girl knew me—from somewhere. Not much of a choice, not really. Prison—or Mars...

BY THE TIME the first policeman reached me, a curious crowd had swung in toward us on all sides, forming a tight little circle. When I move, I move quick. That's what they paid me for at the circus. I wrapped my fingers around the officer's wrist before he knew what had happened, and I wrenched. The blaster tumbled from his hand and he fell away, getting all tangled in the crowd.

His companion tried to do something about it, while everyone started to yell. I don't know if it was an accident or not, but Perez got in the way, and by the time the officer could circumnavigate his ponderous girth, Perez had given me my chance.

I darted into the crowd, pushed my way clear, and sprinted the few remaining feet to the door. It was an eerie feeling, for at any moment I expected to hear the dull roar of a blaster and then hear nothing else at all—ever. Nothing happened, though. Probably fearing they'd hit someone else, the officers had refrained from shooting.

I didn't stop to think about it. Outside, I hustled onto the nearest pedestrian ramp and glided along smoothly with the third fastest level. They couldn't stop all pedestrian traffic on the moving ramps to look for me. That would disrupt the Spaceport's scurrying activity. Oh, they'd do some checking. Maybe they'd even halt ramp ten, the express ramp. But what was so special about ramp eight if a man wanted to escape?

Amnesia is a funny thing. You can go for two or three years without remembering a solitary thing. But then something—like a girl crying a name that must be yours—something can trigger a lost mechanism in your mind. And then things start to move. Not fast, but they move.

Like the nondescript man who'd healed instantly. He'd helped trigger something too, if only I could find it. It gnawed at my consciousness now, an almost physical gnawing. I could feel it trying to break clear of whatever held it in check.

Instantaneous regeneration of injured tissues. Where had I encountered that before? Important? Hell yes! Maybe more important than the beautiful girl who'd uttered the name John Hastings. Regeneration? An asteroid, damn it! Why an asteroid? Don't argue, let it push itself clear. An asteroid—one out of ten thousand… Regeneration, and something secret, so secret that the governments of three worlds would spend half their annual budgets to find out about it. Which mote of an asteriod…

Then I bumped my nose.

The pedestrian ramps swing around the Spaceport like a huge belt, and when you make one complete revolution you're supposed to get off. The bump on the nose was not a gentle reminder, but a tall slender bank of machinery rises out of the ramp at the administration building, running the complicated ribbon of moving roads. That meant a lot of concentrated thinking, and a speeding ramp had carried me around the Spaceport completely, right back to where I started.

I hopped off the ramp quickly, walked around the bank of machinery and got on the other side. I let the ramp carry me half way around this time, out beyond the blasting pits with their gleaming, polished rails and beyond the anti-grav air-docks that housed spaceships.

At that point I left ramp eight for the seventh moving road, left that one for the sixth—working my way down until I reached the first ramp, which hardly moved at all. From there I alighted on the concrete apron that skirts the whole complicated system. And for now, that was it. I didn't doubt that I'd shaken off the police, for I could have left the ramp—and the Spaceport, too—at any one of fifty points.

But I still had to find the girl who knew John Hastings, and that girl was on her way to Mars.

THERE ARE three Spaceport cities in North America. New York for the East, Cedar Rapids for the Midwest, and White Sands for the Far West. There are also three Sargasso Cities.

You know the old legends about sailing ships disappearing in the Sargasso Sea. Well, as far as I know, there's no Sargasso Sea for spaceships, but there are three of them for spacemen.

New York. Cedar Rapids. White Sands. Cities within cities, a hundred taverns and a score of flop houses where ex-spacemen with the wistful look of deep space in their eyes can get a cheap drink and a cheap bed and watch the liners blasting off for Mars or Venus, for the asteroids or the Jovian moons.

Rumors circulate on the twisted, tortuous streets of Sargasso City as freely as Venusian streetwalkers. You can take your pick of the streetwalkers for a stiff shot of Venusian brandy, and the rumor-mongers are just as reasonable. Often, they knew more about a lot of secret things than did the government agents who ventured within Sargasso City to question them. Things like regeneration and asteroids…

And thus it was that I entered Sargasso City with the firm conviction that a lot of talking and a lot more listening might lead to something. Also, in a strictly unofficial sense, Sargasso City was off-limits for the police, and brushing shoulders with murderers and smugglers and political exiles, I'd be able to thumb my nose at the law. Not that I wanted to for any indefinite length of time, but certain things seemed more important than a trumped-up warrant for my arrest.

Sargasso City doesn't merge gradually with Cedar Rapids. It stands off a little to one side, between the city proper and the Spaceport, and when you enter it you have the feeling that you're leaving behind you the morality of our twenty-first century civilization.

IT WAS LATE, after two a.m., but the taverns of Sargasso City never close, except for a brief noontime hour when the floors are wetted down and the debris disposed of. Someone far off in a dusky corner was strumming a ten-stringed Venusian lute as I pushed in through the swinging door of *Port O' No Return Cafe*. A dour little man stood behind the bar, with about as much Japanese blood in him as Venusian upland. The mixture came off olive-green, a little on the pale side.

"Brandy want?" he asked, grinning coarsely. "Or Venus miss? *Port O' No* has both, friend."

I grinned back. "I haven't any money."

The corners of his mouth straightened into a thin line. "Too bad. No money, no nothing. Come again, maybe?"

"Maybe," I said. "Or maybe I'll stay." I took a ring off my finger, gave it to him. I don't know about that ring, I've had it ever since I can remember. I'm no expert, but it looked like Venusian fire opal.

The uplander-Jap gulped, and his Adam's Apple became very prominent. He only looked at the stone for a moment, then said: "One hundred solars, please?"

"It's worth a thousand, and you know it."

"Two hundred is all poor relation can afford. Two hundred?"

I nodded, waited while he counted out the dirty bills and put them in my hand. He asked, "Brandy now or Venus miss?"

I asked for brandy and got it, a good stiff shot—probably what the boys of the old Wild West two hundred years ago would have called three fingers. Only they never heard of Venusian brandy and the kick it carries.

I sipped a little and put the glass down. "What do you know about regeneration?" It wasn't a foolish question, because if he didn't know, someone else here would. I had a distinct hunch this regeneration business carried a wallop as potent as the brandy he served. And Sargasso City wouldn't miss a trick.

"Sorry. Poor relation so idiot. Know nothing. Try professional?"

Sargasso City had professional everythings, from street-walkers to lute players to rumor-mongers. I said I'd be glad to.

"Good. Smart. This way, please."

He called over a mousey-looking girl who scurried behind the bar, picked up a dirty cloth and began to wipe glasses. They didn't look any cleaner when she finished.

"Professional busy-busy. You make appointment?"

I handed over five of the solars. "I'll see him now."

"Other appointment suddenly went cancel," my guide muttered, leading me past a dirty straw mat that hung across the entrance to an alcove. On the other side, there was a desk and two chairs. The breed sat down behind the desk, offered me the other seat. I remained standing, said: "Okay, where's your professional?"

He smiled. "Do not be surprised. I assure you that you are in his presence right now, but if one has to keep up appearances outside, you can forgive that, can you not?" Quite a cultured accent, a bit of Oxford and something of Upland D., and I assure you that the Venus boys coming out of these are no dopes.

"Okay, okay...you fooled me. You're the guy who's supposed—"

"I am a man gifted with something rare enough to make it expensive. Photographic memory, total recall. Please." He extended a hand, and I covered it with solars. "Now, what is it you wish to know about regeneration?"

"Anything you can tell me. A man is struck with a heavy weight, both his arms are broken. Probably some ribs too. A few minutes later he gets up and walks away, as good as new."

"Ahh! I understand. Shall I have your brandy brought in now, Mr. Hastings?"

CHAPTER TWO
Under Martian Moons

I LEANED across the desk and grabbed his dirty white shirtfront. "You'd better talk now," I said. "And fast. Where'd you hear that name?" A card in a pocket, not taken very seriously for a couple of years. Until a girl mentions that name, until someone tries to kill me, until a little uplander-Jap, who happens to have a total-recall memory, mentions the name too. John Hastings.

Me?

"Please, Mr. Hastings. Release me. I abhor violence. My ancestors here on Earth abhorred it too, except for one foolish, abortive mistake back in the last century. My ancestors on Venus likewise detest it, except for a few smaller mistakes, equally abortive. Now, you want to know about regeneration…"

"I want to know about the name John Hastings," I said, releasing him. "Talk!" I think I was a little frightened. I know he wasn't.

"What can I tell you about your own name that you don't already know?" Then the dour face creased into a frown. "Of course. John Hastings disappeared several years ago. Nothing was heard of him, he was assumed to be dead. Now he returns—a victim of amnesia?"

I shrugged hopelessly, said: "Who am I?"

"As I have said, John Hastings. By the gods of Karn, but this is interesting. I have seen pictures of you, but now, in the flesh, after they gave you up for dead...

"John Hastings was an archaeologist who specialized in the asteroids. There is talk, you know, of an ancient civilization that flourished when the asteroids existed as a single unified planet, before they were rent asunder by we know not what."

I told him no, I did not know.

"John Hastings is also a product of Jupiter training. Two-and-a-half gravities to fight in childhood, he became a man of mighty strength, yet he devoted his young life to a strange discipline. Archaeology of the asteroids. Tell me, John Hastings—why?"

Well, they'd billed me as the StrongMan of Jupiter, and there'd been some truth to that, although probably Dufree and the others did not know it. "Better send for that brandy," I said, and the man rang a little bell. I went on, "I don't know a thing about that. Until today, I didn't even know my name was John Hastings. Is there anything else you can tell me?"

"No. You disappeared out among the asteroids, after passing along some hints concerning a startling discovery. A culture old when time was young, an eerie place of ill-remembered life. Ahh...here is the brandy."

I swallowed it in one burning, stinging gulp, and the girl hustled out for some more. "It sure took an awful lot of luck to get me here to you on the first try," I admitted.

HE SHOOK his head deprecatingly. "Not at all. Anyone in Sargasso City knows of John Hastings and the mysteries of space that he almost—but not quite—unfolded. Every now and then an expedition searches the asteroids to look for him. Someone else could have told you the same story.

"But there it ends, for I pieced things together, bit by bit, until I developed a theory concerning you, John Hastings. Would it surprise you if I told you my hobby consists of John Hastings?"

"How's that?"

"You're a legend, a myth. I spend my spare time on that myth. I probably know as much about you as you would know were you not…ill. I hope you don't mind." He smiled politely. "Further, I believe that the disappearance of John Hastings and the mystery of instantaneous regeneration of tissue are directly related. Wait…don't jump to conclusions. Remember, I'm only a hobbyist."

The mousey girl returned with another glass of brandy. "Maybe you'd better tell me all about your hobby," I suggested.

He leaned back, telescoping out one of those long plastic reeds that pass for permanent Venusian cigarettes. He started to say something, I don't know what. Then, outside our little alcove, someone yelped. Other people must have liked the idea, because they took it up and soon the *Port O' No Return* was filled with one roaring din.

The uplander-Jap seemed alarmed. He got up from his chair and crossed rapidly to the straw mat, pulling it aside and peering out. From over his shoulder, I caught a quick glimpse of the chaos—chairs and tables overturned, men and women on the floor, tumbled grotesquely about like rag dolls. At first there seemed no purpose to it all, but organization and planning sometimes has a way of losing itself in a barroom brawl.

Presently a handful of men fought their way toward our alcove, and my companion thrust the hanging back into place, darted to the rear of the alcove, fumbled with a catch on the wall. He didn't make it.

Half a dozen men crowded into the alcove, and before I knew it I was in a fight, a wild, free-swinging affair. Don't ask me why, but there it was. They wanted the uplander-Jap, I stood in the way. And so we fought.

I sent two of them reeling back past the straw hanging, whirled to face a third. Another pair had the uplander-Jap on the floor, squirming and twisting furiously, yelling something in a Venusian dialect. Something—the sort of God-given impulse that can save a jungle animal from destruction—something made me turn around again. From the direction of the ceiling, a heavy chair-leg flashed down. I flung an arm up and felt it go numb as the bludgeon struck, bounced off, descended again. It exploded against the side of my head, threw me to my knees. I tottered that way for a while, saw dimly the uplander-Jap being carted away.

Then I pitched forward on my face, catching the straw hanging with one outstretched hand and bringing it down on top of me. I don't remember hitting the floor...

THE MOUSEY girl was busy applying a cold compress to my temple when I awoke.

"How do you feel?"

"Lousy, thanks."

She was American, a plain sort of kid like the kind you might see working in any soda fountain. Well, you can find anything in Sargasso City.

"They took Togoshira Suuki, you know."

I told her I didn't know. I said, "Who the hell is Suuki?"

"You sat talking with him, so I guessed you were his friend. Suuki, our master."

"Oh, Suuki. Kid, I don't even know what happened."

She withdrew the compress from my temple, looked at me almost haughtily, for all her plainness. "In that case, maybe I'm wasting my time." And just like that she got up to go.

I grabbed her hand and pulled her back. "Hold on a minute. If they took Suuki, I want to get him back." That was the truth. The girl at the sideshow knew me. The girl went to Mars. Suuki knew me, and Suuki was abducted. I think right then I'd have fought my way quite cheerfully through the nine pits of Hell to rescue him.

"Yes," she agreed. "We all loved Suuki." Almost like part of a religious ritual.

"Kid, I'll be frank. I didn't love Suuki. I hardly knew him. But Suuki has something I want and he seemed willing to give it to me—"

"Suuki is benevolent."

"Yeah, sure. Benevolent. Who took him? Why?"

"You mean you don't know?"

"I mean I don't know, that's right. I don't know. I just got into Sargasso City tonight."

"Umm-mm. How can I explain it? You know your history? Remember the Tong wars of Chinatown, New York, a century ago?"

I said I remembered.

"This is much the same, only worse. Sargasso City is more like the old Casbah in Algiers than it is like Chinatown. Here the police do not enter. It is an unwritten law. But there are the same internal clashes for control. Togoshira Suuki rules Sargasso City. Togoshira Suuki represents the Venusian clans." She let it fall like that, staccato, one brief sentence after another. "The Martian clans don't like Suuki. The Martians have taken him…" She held the back of one pudgy hand to her mouth, as if for the first time she realized the extent of the situation.

"Okay, cheer up. When can we start getting him back?"

"You don't understand. They took him where they can keep him safely. They took him to Mars. From there they can dictate terms to the three Sargasso Cities, with Suuki's life in the balance."

YOU HEAR a lot about the Sargasso Cities, how they control the destinies of more than their own squalid environs. It can be overdone, I guess. Government power doesn't rest in the hands of the Tri-World Council. It belongs to the men who rule the Sargasso Cities by gun and knife and wile. Things like that.

I said, "How sure are you they took him to Mars?"

"Don't ask me how I know, you would only waste your breath. But they took him to Mars. Togoshira Suuki."

"Can we go?"

"We? You mean the good folk of Cedar Rapids Sargasso?" She snorted. "It isn't necessary. Our agents on Mars can do the job as well."

Sargasso City—with agents on another planet. My head started to swim a little. That, and a man who could pick himself off the floor with half a dozen broken bones and walk away as good as new a few minutes later. And a cockeyed story about something old and something ancient that held the asteroids together and then blew them apart. And a damned fool named John Hastings who didn't know what was going on and who only found trouble when he tried to find out.

All connected? Neatly, like the pieces of one of those tri-dimensional puzzles that everyone tinkers with these days? Maybe. I didn't know, but I intended to find out. Otherwise, someone else might point his needle gun at my chest some fine day, and next time I might not see it.

I told the mousey kid she could forget about her compresses, I felt fine. Then I asked her if she knew of any way I could get to Mars.

"In a month or two, if you have the money."

"I don't want to wait a month and I haven't got the money."

Suddenly, I found her staring at my head queerly. As if she had seen it for the first time. Some gesture again, back of pudgy hand to mouth.

"That bad?" I grunted, fingering my temple. I felt nothing. No lump, no cut.

"I don't understand. I don't understand. A few minutes ago, you had an ugly gash on your head. Swollen, bleeding— ooo! Now there's nothing. Look, not even a scar."

From somewhere, she got an ornate mirror and held it up for me. Well, she'd exaggerated, because there was a scar. If you looked closely, you could see it, a thin white line. But nothing more. A scar that might have told of a wound several years old and fully healed. I felt fine, too, almost as if nothing had happened.

I scratched my head. "I don't get it, kid." I didn't want to tell her I was thinking of a man who walked away from a three-hundred-pound hit-and-run act without a scratch.

"Togoshira Suuki would understand. The flesh that regenerates itself..." She made that sound like part of a religious ritual too. "Listen! Will you promise to wait right here? Don't go away. Don't move an inch. I'll be back soon."

I nodded, more than a little confused, and she disappeared out through where the straw mat had hung. Some semblance of order had returned to the *Port O' No Return*, but it wasn't very crowded now.

She came back in about half an hour. She looked excited. "They will see you now."

"Who will see me?"

"Don't ask questions. We have no time. You said you wanted to go to Mars, didn't you? To rescue our Suuki?"

THEY SAT in a big room down in the basement of an old dilapidated building across the street from *Port O' No.* Two Earthmen, one stocky, one rapier-thin, both middle-aged. And two Venusians, older, bent and tired, long flowing beards almost flaxen against their deep olive skin.

The mousey girl whispered, "This is the Uplands Brotherhood."

"Uplands, eh? So why two Earthmen?"

"Must you always ask questions? The Brotherhood started out small, and grew. Suuki brought a new purpose to it, and new members. A quarter of a million, all over the Solar System. These four men, with Suuki, are the leaders."

The stocky Earthman grunted something to his companion, then turned to the girl. "This is the man?"

"Yes."

"You're sure about the regen—"

"I am sure."

One of the Venusians stood up, his wobbly legs sheathed in broad, over-sized pantaloons. "He looks like the pictures Suuki has with him! By the gods of Karn, and so he does—like that Earthman, that archaeologist, John Hastings."

More people knew me…

The other Venusian said, "You will swear allegiance to the Brotherhood, naturally."

I shook my head. I didn't know what was going on, but I wasn't going to swear allegiance to anything or anybody, and I told them that.

"That complicates things," the thin Earthman admitted.

"I have my own personal business," I told him. "Your man Suuki happens to be part of it. If you think I can help, I'll try to rescue him, but that's all."

"What is this business?"

Again I shook my head. "Uh-uh. I said personal."

One of the Venusians muttered, in English as good as Togoshira Suuki's: "Don't you understand, boy? If you don't take an oath to us, we can't trust you, not fully. Oh, I won't lie. After Anna's story, we decided you might help us. But it will be limited, for if you don't swear allegiance, we can't tell you everything that could relate to the situation—"

"Nevertheless, I take no oaths." You couldn't blame me.

I'd found myself, found John Hastings, after a couple of years of life without any real personal identity. And life in bondage to an oath might turn out just as odious as the other extreme, life in a kind of vacuum, I wanted no part of it.

The stocky Earthman said, "I'm for forgetting the whole thing. He doesn't trust us, we can't trust him. For all we know, he's in with the Marties—"

The mousey girl, Anna, almost shouted. "Maybe he can bring back Suuki! If he can do that—"

"He'll go," the first Venusian said, "provided he wants to. What do you say, boy?"

"Sure. Sure I want to go. But with no strings attached."

"Fair enough. Are we agreed?" Three heads nodded, and Anna almost jumped up and down. The stocky Earthman sat there growling to himself.

His human companion smiled. "It might work. It just might work. The Marties know our agents, yes—but they don't know you, Hastings. Probably they know *of* you, but so what? Point is, they won't know you're working for us."

"Don't forget," I reminded him. "I'm not. Our plans happen to cross each other, that's all. I want Suuki, you want Suuki. It may not go any further than that. Okay?"

"Okay. But you'll be working pretty much in the dark because of it. Here, take this." The thin Earthman gave me a card, really half a card, yellowish, with nothing written on it.

I turned it over in my hand, scowled. "What's this for?"

"You'll notice it's torn haphazardly. A man on Mars has the other half. They fit, and you're identified."

"How do I get to him?"

"You'll find him in Lake of the Sun City. There's no lake there, and it isn't really a city. Just a dirty little desert town. But that's where you'll find him. He runs a curio shop."

ONE OF the Venusians took it up from there. "Can you leave tomorrow?"

"Huh? Tomorrow? There's no ship out for several weeks…"

"Not out of America, there's not. But a small passenger vessel leaves Rio de Janeiro for the moon, day after tomorrow. A week later, there's a Moon-Mars liner. You'll be on it."

That left some twenty-four hours until I'd have to board the jet for Rio. I soon found that these men of the Brotherhood were not willing to let me out of their sight in that time. A room upstairs over the *Port O' No,* meals brought to me by Anna, who was a faithful lap-dog watchdog combination, because she knew I might find her precious Suuki…

Well, I had some time on my hands and I suppose morbid curiosity got the better of me. I had been struck on the head—hard. Maybe hard enough for a skull fracture. But I healed, almost in a matter of minutes.

Anna brought utensils with my first meal, and they included a small sharp knife. I waited until the girl left my little room. Waited till I heard her footsteps going down the stairs.

Then I toyed with the knife for a few long moments, idly twisting the keen edge around in my fingers.

"What the hell!" I said aloud. "If you want to do it, do it."

I jabbed the point of the knife home, piercing the tip of the index finger on my right hand. A small globule of blood came to the surface, bright red, and I brushed it away. I washed my finger, studied it. No mark. No tiny hole. Nothing.

I tried again, with the same results.

When you're bewildered, you can get angry. More than anything after that, I think I was angry. I used the edge of the knife, cutting an inch-long gash across the back of my forearm.

It hurt, but only for a moment.

It bled—for a moment. I smeared away the blood, then washed it off, scrubbing hard. No cut. Not even a scar.

I had to check a wild impulse to slash the blade across my wrist, across the veins, which bulged when I tightened my fist. Indestructible? I didn't know, but my heart thumped a furious jig inside my chest when I tried to get some sleep.

FOUR HOURS by jet express to Rio. Two days from there to the moon, almost a third of that time spent in the deep acceleration chairs. A checking of credentials at Tycho Station, and that frightened me for a while, but the Brotherhood had given me some neatly forged documents.

Then the Mars rocket, ten days of thumb twiddling. For company, a couple of professors bound for Syrtis Major College, two technicians who thought they could find tritium down near the South Polar cap, half a score of eager tourists, and some Martians, homeward bound. The Marties kept pretty much to themselves, as Marties generally do.

I didn't realize my mistake until we landed at Syrtis Major. The usual quarantine followed, while we were sprayed with antibiotics to ward off Martian diseases that otherwise would encroach upon virgin territory with a nasty insistence. I made my way from the lab to the men's locker room to pick up my gear, and something made me look through one of the aft ports. I don't know what, call it an impulse, call it a hunch—but I looked.

The Marties were leaving, five of them with their dry, parchment-like skin and stooped shoulders. They carried something, a large crate, depositing it on a waiting sand-sled. With it they whisked away across the rust desert.

Just like that, only I'd been an idiot to end all idiots!

Sure, the Brotherhood had spoken of Suuki being taken to Mars. They'd spoken in the past tense, as if it were already an accomplished fact. Except that the Moon-bound ship from Rio was the first vessel off Earth, and the Luna-Mars rocket the first one to reach the red planet…

Which meant Togoshira Suuki had been abducted right under my nose!

I'd brushed against the polite, aloof Marties a dozen times on shipboard. They'd had Suuki trussed up in the baggage room all that time. I sighed wearily as I got back into my clothing. I guess I wasn't cut out to be an undercover man.

Outside, the cold desert winds whipped in over the Spaceport like howling demons, and when you haven't been on Mars for a while, your first breath of Martian air always makes you think you're going to strangle. You get used to it after a time, though, and if you keep exertion down to a minimum, you can get along well enough.

I asked the Martian female at the travel desk if she knew anything about the Marties who'd just left the ship. She was polite, but she was adamant.

"Earth sir, you know we are not permitted to divulge such information."

I frowned. "You haven't answered my question."

"Then, if I must, no."

"Well, where did they go?"

Borrowing a mannerism from the Earth tourists, she shrugged her bony shoulders. She was young, maybe ten Martian years—roughly twenty years old, Earth style—but she didn't look it. I think even Martian infants must look senile, although I've never seen a Martian infant. Mostly, it's the skin, dry and wrinkled and withered from birth. "Again, Earth sir, I don't know. They had a private sled waiting for them, as you may have observed. Now, can I arrange transportation for you?"

"Yes. I'd like to reach Lake of the Sun City as soon as possible."

"That is a long trip across the desert."

"I know Martian geography. When can I go?"

"There is a helicopter in five days—"

"Five days! I haven't the time."

"A sand-sled today, if you want it."

"Sure," I said. I didn't like the idea of a bumpy ride across the rust deserts by sand-sled, the jets kicking up a fine spray of sand that makes you half-suffocate. But I'd arrive in Lake of the Sun City in two days that way, and I was in a hurry. Suuki was one thing, but I hadn't forgotten the girl who'd called my name at the sideshow, triggering off everything with it. I kept a special place in my Martian itinerary for her...

The Martian clerk jabbed a long finger at a bell on her desk, rang it. In a moment, a scrawny Martian appeared, removing his cowl and glancing quizzically at us.

"Yes?"

"This Earth sir would like you to take him to Lake of the Sun City—at once."

"At once," said the Martie. "Of course. One hundred solars."

The Brotherhood had stuffed my pockets with money, and I reached in for a hundred-solar note and gave it to him. He pocketed the bill greedily, then motioned for me to follow him outside.

The jet sled is ten feet long, maybe twelve. You sit up front, the driver sits behind you at the controls. In that way, he gets the brunt of the jet-spray, but the prow of the sled dips in and out of the red Martian sands with the thrust of half a dozen obsolete jets, and the ride is one choking, coughing torment.

But fast, for the Martian barrens present a surface more level than Earth's Daytona Beach or the salt flats of Utah. A hundred miles an hour is average, one-fifty is not really exceptional, and on wide-open stretches some sand-sleds have been known to pass the two-century mark. Add that speed to the thin Martian air, and you have a problem. You simply can't breathe the tenuous air fast enough to stay alive.

THE MARTIANS have solved it like they solve everything else. Secretly. No one quite understands the mechanism, but you're given a sort of insulated leather pouch. Some say it holds a combination of liquid oxygen and inert gasses. I don't know. All I know is this: you hold the pouch down near your waist with a long plastic straw protruding from its top, and you sip through that straw, somehow sucking up air—no longer liquid, no longer cold— and breathing through your mouth. The pouch is fastened around your neck with a thong of leather, but you'd better hold it tightly, for you'd be an oxygen-starved wreck in a matter of minutes without it.

Anyway, I found myself zooming across the flat Martian tundra on a sand-sled. Behind me I could hear the wheezing sound that passed for breathing among the Martians. The desert sands roared up from the horizon and then swept away on both sides, and when some of the fierce Martian winds blew the wrong way I could get a quick whiff of the acrid jet fumes.

Late morning gave way to early afternoon, and we stopped to eat some dried beef from Earth, washing it down with precious Martian water. Then my Martie grumbled something, and we were on our way again.

A chill wind crept up in the late afternoon, and by sunset it grew cold. Well, in half an hour or so we'd reach one of the way stations and spend the night there, underground. Soon I could see it looming out of the darkness, a small opaque dome with a beacon light blinking on and off atop it.

The Martian did not stop.

I turned to stare at him, but he had his head tucked deep down inside his cowl. I tried to yell something above the roaring wind, gave it up as useless. The cold knifed in and I grew numb, felt the plastic straw slipping from my lips. I bit into it grimly, held it there with my teeth. The Martie could have been laughing. I thought I heard him, but probably the wind was playing tricks.

So numb…and stiff…

Hands probed at the back of my neck, suddenly. I tried to fight them off, found it difficult to move. Soon the leather thong dropped down over my shoulders. Something prodded the leather pouch that had fallen to my lap. It teetered there for a moment, then fell away, slowly, end over end, as in a frozen dream…

We sped on, and I began to choke—

I don't know for how long, but I did not lose consciousness, not entirely. And after a time the sled screeched to a stop. Soon I'd be able to breathe again, and when I got my hands on that damned Martie…

I felt myself rolled over helplessly, off the sled. I lay there gazing up at the Martian moons, Deimos no more than a bright star, Phobos a tiny sliver of light off near the horizon.

The Martie was a dim bulk in the darkness, kneeling by my side and laughing. I reached up feebly, stiff with cold, weak with suffocation, and he thrust my hands away, leaned over my chest.

He held a knife, its polished blade barely visible by Phobos-light. Would it all end, then, so soon—under the pale moons of Mars, with the light of Phobos gleaming faintly off a long steel blade? A crazy thought, but it hammered over and over again at my brain; it wasn't fair. I knew so little of everything, of myself most of all.

I felt the knife slip in, slowly. He must have taken great pleasure from it. Grating against my ribs, sliding in between them, twisting...

I think I screamed once, and that was all.

CHAPTER THREE
Regeneration

"HE'S WAKING."

"Impossible! He should have died two weeks ago. Frozen stiff out on the desert, a knife hilt-deep in his chest—"

"See for yourself."

"I see, but I—"

Voices in a swirling vortex of sound, fading and coming closer, fading again. I tried to sit up, but someone pushed me down.

"Take it easy, young man! You died once, you know, as far as I can tell. Why don't you live a bit more slowly this time?"

One minute. Two. I began to feel better. Three, four. Almost strong again. After five minutes, I sat up. I was hungry, and I told them.

Two white-garbed men stood there, one scratching his bald head, the other turning away, plainly frightened.

"How do you feel, son?"

"Fine. But hungry. Man, I'm hungry."

A nurse came in with some instruments. They took my blood pressure. They fluoroscoped me. They listened to my heartbeat. They did five or six other things that doctors always do.

The bald man said, "He's well."

"He's *what?*"

"Well. Healed. All better. We could discharge him today—if we didn't want to study him."

"Wait a minute! I've been a doctor forty years. They find this man out on the desert a couple miles from one of the way stations. He has no heartbeat. He's frozen solid, like a block of ice. They take him to the morgue here in Syrtis Major and he starts to warm up. His heart begins to beat, feebly. They pull the knife out. Next day the wound disappears, a thin white scar taking its place.

"Okay. Okay! That can't happen, but we saw it for ourselves. Estimate—two weeks on the desert. Warm days, sub-zero nights. No food. No water. Probably not even breathing in all that time. Somehow, his body forgets to decompose.

"We bring him here. And that was yesterday. Today, he opens his eyes for the first time. He sits up, says he's hungry. A few minutes pass, and he's fit as a fiddle. Elkins, I'm scared."

"Listen," I said, "my name is Hastings. John Hastings. Does that mean anything?"

The frightened old man in surgeon's gown shook his head, hardly listening. The other doctor, Elkins, was still scratching the bald spot atop his head. "Does it mean anything? Hastings? I'll say! Did you hear that? He said he's John Hastings…"

"HASTINGS? HASTINGS? *Hastings!*" The older doctor sat down on the foot of the bed, cupping his head in his hands. "John Hastings died three years ago out among the asteroids. They found his ship, a gutted ruin. Full of food and full of water. He could have taken none of it with him, and he disappeared. How do you live on the asteroids without food and water, not to mention air?"

Elkins smiled. "Hastings did a pretty good job of it on our Martian desert, don't you think?"

"I don't know what to think. I don't know. I almost wish they'd never found him. It isn't easy to throw forty years of learning out the window. Here's a man who should have died twice, not probably, but definitely. Only he looks strong as an ox."

I didn't know what was going on, but I laughed. "And hungry," I reminded them.

Elkins sent the nurse out for some food, then turned to me: "Son, how would you like to stay on here for a few months?"

"You said I was well."

"And you are. But when medical science finds something like this, it wants to study! Also, maybe you can tell us what happened out among the asteroids. It's been quite a mystery, you know."

"Don't ask me. I don't remember a thing. I don't even remember being an archaeologist. About all I know right now is this: my name is John Hastings. When people find that out, they make a big fuss. But the answer to your question, doctor, is no."

"No? You can't refuse!"

"Sorry. I'm going to."

"Wait. When you said you remember nothing, does that mean you have amnesia? Loss of memory, is that what you mean?"

I nodded, dug into the food when it was brought.

"In that case, you've *got* to stay on! With the new hypnotic treatment we could probably restore your memory."

"Probably, eh? How long will it take?"

"Depends on you, Hastings. Six months is a good figure."

"Not for me it isn't. I haven't got six months to spend on it, doc. Maybe some day, if things work out the way I want them to, I'll tell you the whole story. That is, if I ever learn it myself."

IT'S THINKING, and I came to the conclusion that the man who ran the curio shop in Lake of the Sun City, or enigmatic Suuki, or the girl who'd first spotted me—any of these might turn out a lot quicker than hypnotic treatment. "Where's my clothing, doc?"

"You mean you'll leave? We can't be responsible. You might have a relapse—"

"I doubt it."

"Frankly, so do I. As for your clothing, uh-uh. It was frozen solid. We had to peel it off you in strips. You'll have to get some new duds, I'm afraid."

I jumped out of bed. "Say…did you find anything?"

"In your clothing, you mean? Yes, we did. A thousand solars, also ruined. We've turned them in to the government, and you'll be reimbursed."

"Nothing else?"

"Like what?"

"Like half of a little card?"

Elkins shook his head. "No. Nothing."

"Nuts," I grumbled. "There goes Lake of the Sun City and a guy who maybe could have helped me."

"I don't know what you're talking about, Hastings, but is there anything I can do?"

"No. No, thanks. Wait—hold on a minute. Just how much of a big-wig are you around these parts?"

Elkins smiled. "I'm chief surgeon here in Syrtis Major Hospital. That makes me the ranking medical man on Mars."

"Well, those thousand solars are yours if you can do something for me."

"I don't want your money, Hastings. But this whole thing does intrigue me. Submit to our treatment and I'll do what I can."

I said no at once. "That wouldn't work. The whole idea is for me to save time, and the treatment would delay me. How's this for a compromise? If I ever get this whole mess straightened out, I'll tell you. I'll let you know all about it—if I'm still alive."

Elkins chuckled softly. "I don't think you could die even if you wanted to! Okay, it's a deal. What can I do for you?"

"Just this. About a month ago, the *Martian Queen* left Cedar Rapids for Mars. Have you access to the passenger list?"

He told me he could get it.

"Good. Bring it to me, along with copies of the passport pictures. There's a girl—"

"Yes, sir..." Elkins grinned. "Yes, *sir!*"

I said something about not meaning to order him around, but he laughed. I think he was enjoying the whole thing.

I TOOK a room in the *Red Sands Hotel,* and that night Elkins came to me with two things. First, he had a packet of money—one thousand solars, which the Earth government office in Syrtis Major had passed along for me in return for the thousand ruined solars. Second, he had the passenger list, complete with pictures.

It took less than a minute. "That's her," I said, jabbing a finger at one of the photographs.

"Pretty little thing," Elkins mused. And I agreed. A tumbled mass of chestnut hair, a pert little nose, sparkling blue eyes, the suggestion of a dimple in one cheek.

"Here's her bio," Elkins said, handing me a sheet of paper. I read:

Crewson, Ellen. Age, 25. Height, 5' 5". Weight, 120. Color of Eyes, blue. Associate Professor of Archaeology, Syrtis Major College. Appointed June last. References, check President Matthew P. Ryder, S.M.C. Period of stay on Mars, indefinite.

Bright and early the next morning, I found myself walking along the campus lanes of Syrtis Major College. Most of the students I observed were Marties, but a fair sprinkling of Earth youth could be seen, and an occasional Venusian shivered inside his furs, struggling against the unfamiliar cold of the Martian desert.

At the registrar's office they told me where I might find Associate Professor Ellen Crewson. It seemed she would be eating breakfast at the Campus Coffee Shop, very much an Earth-sounding name for a Martian college.

I found her, too—or rather, she found me. As I pushed in through the door she jumped up at once from a nearby booth and gave a little squeal of joy. "John!" she cried. "It really *is* you, John Hastings!"

Just like that, she leaped into my arms. A good leap and a strong one, and it nearly carried me over backwards. Then her arms were about my neck and she was kissing me, sobbing all the while. I must have reacted clumsily, for soon she disengaged herself and began to blush. She still held on to my hand, leading me back to the booth and plunking down beside me.

"I—I'm sorry," she said. "You don't remember, do you?"

I shook my head. "From the way you act, I think I'd like to remember."

THAT DEEPENED the blush on her pretty face, but when she smiled, the dimple I'd seen in the picture seemed more pronounced. "Tell me, were you that—that Bok-kura in the sideshow?"

"Uh-huh, that was me."

"I knew you were on Mars. All the morning papers carried it; how they found you out on the desert, how they took you to the hospital, how—"

"All the papers?"

"You bet. Front page stuff, too. You're pretty famous, John. I don't know a professor here at the college who wouldn't give his right arm to talk to you."

"That's no good. The last thing I'd want is publicity. If all the newspapers feature it, my enemies will know, too."

"You sound so melodramatic. Your enemies? Who?"

I shrugged. "I wish I knew, Miss Crewson. I wish I knew."

She began to giggle, softly at first, and then she was laughing quite heartily.

"What the hell's so funny?"

"Miss Crewson, you said. Miss Crewson! Would you believe that a couple of years ago you were on the verge of proposing? Miss Crewson..." The giggling turned to sniffling.

I felt a lot like a would-be strong man trying to clean-and-jerk his first barbell. "I'm sorry," I said. "I remember… nothing. And say, Miss Crew—Ellen—that's why I'm on Mars. I want you to tell me what you know. Everything."

"I'm a dope," she told me. "A real first-rate dope. It looks like I've been carrying the torch for you all this time, and you don't even remember. What am I supposed to do now, just—"

"Hey! It's not that way at all. Didn't you read the papers? I haven't forgotten you alone of everything. I *forgot*. The works. The boys at the hospital call it amnesia."

"Don't mind me," she replied. "I said I was a dope. Of course, I should have known."

"Ellen, how well did you know John Hastings? And don't mind if I speak in the third person that way. John Hastings still sounds like something out of a storybook to me."

She pouted. "I knew him better than anyone else did. I knew him well enough for him to ask me—"

WE WERE getting no place fast. Every time she thought of the past, she thought of her love for John Hastings. And while looking at her I could readily see why the vague and shadowy John Hastings could have returned that love, still, right now I had other things on my mind. I drove that point home, ruthlessly. I had to.

"Sorry," she said, sitting up very straight. "We'll forget all that, John. Now, what do you want to know?"

"Like I said: everything. Where was John Hastings going before he disappeared? What was he looking for? Did he find it? What happened to him? Did he let you know anything about regeneration of tissues or something like that? Did he—"

"Whoa! I see what you mean. Everything. You know what I think?"

"What?"

"I think I'm going to cut my classes today and give the students a day off. There's a park I know down by one of the old canal beds. We can take a picnic lunch there and I'll keep on talking until you run out of questions. Fair enough?"

I told her that would be fine, said I'd meet her at the park by twelve-thirty. Then I strolled back leisurely across the campus and into Syrtis Major City. Picking up a couple of newspapers, I brought them up to my room and ordered a pot full of coffee and some donuts, Earth-style. I began to read.

By the time the coffee had arrived, I was cursing Dr. Elkins volubly. Damn the man! In his enthusiasm to get everything across to all the people who wanted to hear the latest episode in the John Hastings mystery, he'd really spilled the works. The esoteric John Hastings had turned up on Mars. Dead, but then he came back to life. He didn't remember much, but he had a lead. Associate Professor Ellen Crewson of S.M.C. The readers were advised to wait for startling developments, for Miss Crewson, it seemed, had been close to John Hastings years ago, before everything started to happen.

I thought I'd call Elkins and tell him what he could do with those newspapers. But I reconsidered. Looking back on it, I knew I hadn't told him to keep anything a secret. So it wasn't really his fault—but that didn't matter much. Point was, he'd probably opened the floodgates of trouble.

I put a call through to Ellen Crewson, waited. In five minutes the operator called back, told me Miss Crewson hadn't been seen by her Martian landlady all morning. Alarmed now, I got the address from the college, took one more mouthful of coffee and went downstairs.

ALL MARTIANS look withered and old, but the landlady of Ellen Crewson's boarding house seemed old even for a Martie. Her wrinkled, folded skin could have passed for coarse burlap, her rheumy eyes squinted out from two cavernous holes above her cheekbones.

"Miss Crewson," I said. "I called a few minutes ago."

"Not here." Her voice was the shadow of a croak.

"Do you know where I can find her?"

"No message."

"I said, do you know where I can find her?"

"No."

"When did you see her last?"

"Don't remember."

I took out a fifty-solar note, gave it to her. "When did you see her last?"

"Forty, fifty minutes ago, she leave."

"Alone?"

"No."

It was like pulling wisdom teeth with your bare hands. "With who?"

"Man."

Fifty more solars changed hands. "Who was he?"

"Not of Earth."

"A Martian?"

"No."

"Damn it, then who?"

"Venus-man. She go out with big Venus-man. She look plenty scared, yes."

"Why the hell didn't you try to stop them? Why didn't you call the police?"

"No one tell me to. Big Earthman take her—"

"I thought you said Venusian!"

"Venus-man, yes. Sorry. He—"

I placed my hands on her shoulders, and it felt as if nothing but the tattered cloak covered her bones. I shook her and she made a rattling noise. "You got all the money you're going to get! Now, who was it?"

She cackled. "I fool you for a time, yes?"

"Who was it?"

"Martian man take her. Remove hands, please. Ahh—better!"

"Did you know the man? Wait. Before you answer, consider this: if I think you're not telling me the truth, I'm going to call the police. Now, did you know him?"

A pause, then: "Live down street. Three brooders. Oldest take her. Two brooders sleeping there now, work nights. You find." She mumbled the address. "Now go from here. Earthfellow?"

"Yes," I said. "I'm going. But I'll be back if you lied."

"No lie. Brudders hate Earth-fellow. Hate Venus-man too, but hate Earth-fellow better. They kill you in little slices. Goodbye."

I used her phone to call the police. I told them that Ellen Crewson was missing, but I did not mention the three brothers. The police would find that out for themselves in due time, and meanwhile I wanted to call on the brothers—undisturbed.

THE PLACE stank. More a shack than a house, it squatted bore and ugly between two sandstone buildings. It smelled of liquor, the Martian rot-gut that can make Earth moonshine taste like tea. It smelled also of unbathed Martians, but I wasn't aware of that until I threw open the door and strode I inside.

Two Martians sat up in their cots, blinking at me. When one spoke it surprised me, especially after the old hag's pidgeon-English.

"All right, wise guy, just who the hell do you think you are busting in here like that?" Thick and heavy-set for a Martian, he sounded like he'd be aggressive even in his sleep. The other one, the younger of the two, seemed more than willing to let his brother do all the talking.

I said, "I'm looking for the other one. There are three of you, aren't there?"

The thickset Martian got up and lit an Earth cigarette. He gestured at the empty third cot. "He ain't here."

"I can see that. Where can I find him?"

"You with the police?"

Maybe the old hag could give me the run-around, but not these boys. I took a quick step toward the Martie and hit him, not really hard, but hard enough to jar him. He fell back with the blow and sat down on his cot, but his brother jumped up like an uncoiled spring.

I hit him, too. Harder. He fell down and he lay there on the floor, breathing hard. I was plenty sore, at myself as much as anyone else. I felt responsible for Ellen Crewson and Ellen might be anywhere...

"Before I'm finished you'll wish I was the police," I said.

"Where's your brother?"

"Braaak!" The chunky Martian stuck his tongue out and made a loud blubbering noise with his lips.

His brother came off the floor fast, with a knife. I've got fast reflexes—they paid me for that, as Bok-kura. I kicked it out, caught his wrist with my foot, and sent the knife clattering across the dirty floor. By the time it struck the wall, I had the Martian down on his face, my knee pressing against the small of his back. I forced his right arm up behind him until he began to yell.

"Now talk!"

The other Martian was shouting. "Hold your horses, bud! He can't speak a word of English. Me, I worked fifteen years in the New York Spaceport, but he don't know the lingo." The Martie tensed, ready to spring for the doorway, but I had his brother on the floor just this side of the threshold, and he thought better of it.

"Okay, then you talk; or do you want me to break his arm?"

HE HADN'T give up yet. He looked furtively across the room at the knife. "Hold it," I said. "Make a move in that direction and your brother will be wearing a lot of plaster for a long time."

That stopped him. The Martians are notoriously clannish, and he'd have felt the broken arm as much as his younger brother.

"The third one," I repeated. "Where is he?"

"He ain't here."

I made his brother scream.

"All right, cut it out!" New York slang, sure enough, almost twentieth-century variety. It sounded strange from the thin lips of a Martian. "Our brother left for the desert this morning."

"It's a mighty big desert," I informed him.

"Lake of the Sun City, that's where he went."

"Not alone. Don't try to tell me he went alone."

"I didn't say nothing. He had a girl with him, an Earth girl. That's all I know, honest, Mr. Hastings."

His mistake was in using my name. If he knew me, then maybe he was in on the whole thing. In that case, he could warn the Marties at Lake of the Sun City in advance.

I let the other brother up and he scrambled off the floor, threw himself down on a cot and began to sob. The thickset Martie brought him some wine in a dark leather pouch, and he gulped it greedily.

I said, "Have you got a sled?"

"Yeah, sure. That's our business. Sledding."

"We're going to use it, the three of us. Right now."

"Where we going?"

"I'm going to Lake of the Sun City. Okay, where's the sled?"

"Right out back. I guess we can start now, but I don't like it. I got a lotta business signed up for tonight, on acounta this is the only all-weather sled in the neighborhood. You can't just—"

"I can and I am, so don't waste your breath." The Marties didn't know it, of course, but I was angry enough to kill someone at that moment.

We went out together through the doorway, walked around behind the shack. I looked at the sand-sled and smiled. It seemed all set to go, complete with half a dozen breathing bags. Three big metal hoops trisected its length, too. Covered with stout leather, they could offer considerable protection against the night's cold. And that meant I could drive straight through to Lake of the Sun City without a stop. Well, just one stop...

I had the Marties bring along plenty of dried meat and a canteen of water. I wouldn't be sitting with my back to any Martians on a sand-sled, not this time. I had them give me instructions concerning the controls, and we were all set to go.

Driving through the crooked streets of Syrtis Major, I got used to the jet sled. Actually, there wasn't much to it. One lever for starting and accelerating, one for braking, one for turning. By the time we left the city behind us, I had the sled zooming over the sands of Mars at a good clip.

We'd done better than a hundred fifty miles in the first hour, and then I stopped. "Climb out," I told the Martians.

"What do you mean?"

"You walk from here. You can walk back to Syrtis, you can walk seventy miles to the nearest way-station." I jabbed a finger at the parchment map and showed them our approximate location.

"I thought you was taking us along—"

I grunted something, watched them trudge away from the sled. They'd fare all right. A Martian can go a long while without food or drink. Meanwhile, I'd reach Lake of the Sun City long before they could give any warning.

As I remember it, I was feeling pretty sure of myself then. The older brother was taking Ellen to Lake of the Sun City. If mayhem had been on his mind, a jaunt across the desert would be meaningless. Togoshira Suuki's Brotherhood had mentioned Lake of the Sun City as a key point, too. Thus, it looked like I might be able to tie things together for the first time out at the ancient Martian town, which some say once was the capital of a mighty Martian empire.

CHAPTER FOUR
Lake of the Sun

THE DOOR to the curio shop tinkled as I opened it, like any door on an Earth curio shop might tinkle. The proprietor was all smiles and politeness, a young Martian woman who might have had some Earth blood in her veins. I couldn't be sure, but the mixture often comes off Mongoloid, and she almost could have been a daughter of one of Genghis Khan's Noyons.

"Yes, sir?" she said, in more than passable English. That's one thing about travel on Mars or Venus. If you stay on the well-beaten tourist trails, you won't have any language difficulties. I suppose the natives know on which side their bread is buttered. The girl continued, "Ours is the only curio shop in Lake of the Sun City. Here you will find items of last—"

"I know all that. Sorry, but I'm not interested."

The smile was a fixture on her face. "What then, Earth sir?"

"In Cedar Rapids Sargasso, I met a Venusian named Togoshira Suuki. He was abducted. His friends thought I might be able to find him, so they sent me here."

"I don't know what you're talking about."

"Look. First, Suuki was abducted. I came to look for him, got an Earth girl named Ellen Crewson involved, and they took her too. I'm here to look for both of them, and I won't take no for an answer."

The smile still lingered on her lips. "I am Gurra dor Beta. I run a simple, honest business, and when I do business with someone, he calls me Beta. If you have business with me, you may call me that, but if you do not, I wish you would leave."

"They gave me half a card, but I lost it. Maybe you read the papers, I don't know. I'm John Hastings—"

For the first time, Gurra dor Beta looked doubtful. "Hastings! If I dared believe… Have you any proof?"

"No. But there's an old picture of me in the papers."

Wordless, she scurried through an archway, returned in a moment with the *Syrtis Major Chronicle*. Finally, she extended her hand. "It's not a very good likeness, John Hastings, but you're the man. What can I do to help?"

"I don't know," I admitted. "They merely told me to contact you. But this may be a lead. There are three brothers in Syrtis Major City; one of them speaks English like a man from the slums of New York. They run a jet-sled business…"

"I know them! The brothers Karnjud. What have they got to do with it?"

"The oldest brother took Miss Crewson from Syrtis Major and brought her here. I have a hunch he'd also know where to find Suuki."

"Perhaps. We've thought for a long time that Karnjud tor Ig—I guess you'd call him Ig Karnjud—we've thought that he worked with the Martian League."

"LET'S GET this straight. Upland Brotherhood on Venus. Martian League—and I suspect regeneration fits in there someplace too. What's going on?"

"Don't you know?"

And, after I shook my head: "It's quite simple. Rumor had it that John Hastings discovered the secret of regeneration of tissues. The three planet governments have scoffed at it openly, but they've worked furiously in secret to either confirm or refute the rumor. Think about it, those who control regeneration control the Solar System. What are injuries to an army? A man is hurt, he heals. He loses an arm, he'll grow a new one. He dies, and regeneration brings him back to life again.

"And that isn't all. Who is to say that a man whose tissues regenerate themselves is not gifted with eternal life? Tissues run down, fail to replace parts, become old and useless. Senility results. But what if those tissues continuously recreated themselves, remaining young and hardy—*always?*"

My tongue stuck to the roof of my mouth, but I managed the one word, "Immortality!" *I* healed like that. Me, John Hastings! I didn't know why, I didn't know how—but I'd seen it happen. *And did that mean I'd somehow been vouchsafed a veritable godhood?*

"…so, John Hastings, if you can tell me—"

"It's true," I said. "At least, I think it's true. Regeneration exists somehow, somewhere. Suuki thought that, didn't he?"

"Of course. The Brotherhood thinks so. Also the Martian League."

"Where do you fit in?" I wanted to know. "I mean, you're a Martian, yet you work with the Brotherhood."

"My grandmother was a woman of Earth. Her son, my father—lived his life on Venus. It is only natural—"

"You have a Martian name," I persisted.

"I wouldn't be an effective undercover agent without one, would I? Anyway, we stray from the subject. What can I do?"

"That's simple. Just tell me where I can find your friend Iggy."

"Who? Oh, Karnjud tor Ig! And he's no friend of mine. Well, the Martian League preys on the superstitions of the Martian people. Karnjud tor Ig is a sort of priest, and he does a good job of it. They mix science with religion, satisfying the people but still getting out of it what they want. Probably he'll make a religious fiend of Suuki, and one of your Earth girl as well. He'll torture them, extract the information he desires—and the Martians will approve. The Martians will get Suuki and the girl after that..."

"All right. When?"

"Tonight... The nearer moon goes through its phases rapidly, and the moon is now full. A night for the Elder Gods of Mars, John Hastings. A night for the cults to assemble in Lake of the Sun. A night for mystery and the ancient rites—and death."

"You say Lake of the Sun like there really was a lake. I thought it dried up thousands of years ago and only the old name remained to tell of it."

"Lake of the Sun never disappeared! Fed by underground streams, it once covered this entire desert basin, more an ocean than a lake. But the air of Mars grew thin and Mars was parched. The old Martians hollowed out the caverns whose streams fed Lake of the Sun, and you'll find the lake there. Underground. A lake not of the sun now, but of the nether regions into which the sun's rays never penetrate. It is funny. Lake of the Sun…"

"Not so funny for Suuki or Ellen Crewson," I told her. "How do I get there?"

"You don't. They'd kill an Earthman on sight if they caught him during those rites. You're halfway around the planet from Syrtis Major, John Hastings, and Earth law doesn't reach this far. May I make a suggestion?" I nodded. She continued. "Good! I said you cannot go, and that is true. But a Martian could."

"You don't mean yourself?"

"Not alone, no. But I will join you. *You* will go, John Hastings, but you will be a Martian."

SHE WASN'T kidding. She led me through the archway, returned for a moment to the outside room, closing her shop for the day. Then she went to work, and she was an expert.

She injected a bubbling, frothy stuff high up on my right arm, piercing the veins near the armpit with her needle. I felt nothing more than a little giddiness, but when she let me look in a mirror, John Hastings didn't scowl back at me!

Parchment-like skin. Dry, withered, almost ready to flake off.

"My God!" I cried. "This isn't permanent, is it?"

"No, stop worrying. Twenty hours and you will be normal again. Meanwhile…"

Next, she applied a sort of flesh-like putty to my face, building the cheekbones high and gaunt, developing the brow, making the chin protrude. A drop of liquid in each eye, and I found I had to squint like any sand-blown Martian.

Beta stood back with hands on hips, surveying her work. "You will pass," she said, almost proudly, very much the master artist. "Now, all we'll have to find for you is a smelly old cloak, a tattered cowl, a little information on the local customs…"

I told her I hoped the boys at Lake of the Sun would fall for it too.

They did. After sundown, Beta and I entered an unimposing little cave and started down a long winding tunnel. I got the impression that the way led us deep into the bowels of Mars, for although the slope was gradual, it never leveled off.

High up in niches in the wall, flambeaux lighted our way, showing quite clearly the scores of Martians who plodded down the tunnel with us, cowls set low over their faces, shoulders hunched. Moisture dripped off the walls, made the rough stone floor slippery underfoot. Dank, subterranean. moisture—on arid Mars!

Ahead, I became aware of a faint, faraway chanting; almost one with the dripping of water. Eagerly, Beta shuffled forward, and the uneven rock flooring gave way to a spongy carpet of moss. The flambeaux no longer lighted our way— but we could see, for a strange glow filled the air, dancing motes eddying around the unseen currents of wind.

ABRUPTLY, the tunnel opened out into a huge cavern. The further wall was lost in dimness, the ceiling hid behind a veil of the dancing motes. Hordes of Martians streamed in from other passages, gathering together at the shore of an iridescent lake.

Lake of the Sun…

The tiny glowing motes, which had given light to our path, streamed up from the surface of the lake! Lake of the Sun, indeed, with a million, million tiny suns gleaming up from its still depths!

The Martians clustered on the lakeshore, chanting and beating their feet against the rock, rapt eyes intent upon the surface of the waters. We joined them, Beta and I, and my guide knew the chant, lending her own voice to it, stamping her feet in slow cadence. I think I felt more completely the intruder than any man who'd ever set foot on a far planet.

Something sparkled far out on the glowing lake, then came closer. A barge, big and squat and riding low in the water. On it three figures.

Not until the barge drifted in some fifty yards away did I see them clearly. A Martian, tall for his race and strong, and I heard Beta whisper, "That's Ig Karnjud!" And two others, bound to a pole that rose up from the center of the barge.

Dour Togoshira Suuki. And Ellen Crewson.

Ig Karnjud raised his hands on high. The chanting faded away, and only the gentle lapping of water against the barge's hull broke the impossible silence.

Karnjud's voice boomed out across the cavern. I turned to Beta and said, "What's he saying?"

"Shh! He asks if anyone would speak before the ritual begins. And I would speak!" She cried out across the waters in Martian, her voice a plaintive wail. Cowled Marties stirred restlessly all about us.

I didn't understand a word of it, not the old Martian dialect. But wildly I realized my own name had been spoken. John Hastings, she called that out to the still figures in the barge!

Rough hands grabbed me, tore the cowl from my head, ripped the robes from my body. I stood there in jumper and leatheroid jacket, and Beta was laughing! "Fool!" she cried. "Fool, fool! Did you think for a moment that I would help? Did you in your vanity conclude that I—"

I WASN'T listening. She'd tricked me, utterly. No longer wrinkled and withered and parchment-yellow—my skin was the skin of an Earthman! She'd gained my confidence, given me a disguise to quell my doubts completely—then led me to the slaughter. Suddenly the words of the members of the Brotherhood came back to me. A *man* would be waiting in Lake of the Sun City with the other half of my torn card. A man! Somehow, the Martians had put one of their own in his place.

I grabbed the cowl of the nearest Martian, tugged him close, and lifted him overhead. He was screaming when I hurled him at his fellows, and for a moment they cowered back, licking their wounds. Beta still laughed.

They came for me slowly, creeping up on all sides, in no great hurry. They seemed to relish every moment of it. Or perhaps no one wanted to reach me first.

You always gain a momentary advantage if you do the unexpected. I didn't wait for them. Instead, I hurled myself forward, came into contact with the vanguard of their rank— flailed my way through. Panting, I stood on the edge of the lake, my back to its silent waters. I turned away and dove into the gleaming wetness, felt it close around me.

I broke surface, gasped a lung full of the moist air and set out in a crawl for the barge. The water hissed violently all about me, great jets of steam puffing off its surface. Some of the Marties had blasters!

I dived under, employing a frog kick and breaststroke. The water, gleaming with its endless tiny motes of light offered almost no visibility, but far ahead a vague shadow led me on. The barge, I hoped. No Marties came swimming after me, and I soon realized that none would. Few are the desert nomads who can swim, and Mars is an arid wasteland of a planet.

My head spun, my chest burned for air, but I could imagine the Marties waiting patiently on shore with their blasters, and I did not come up for air. If I could swim around behind the barge, if only I could do that.

First, the Marties would have no target to shoot at, and that would suit me fine. Also, Ig Karnjud would wait for me on the shoreward side of the barge. Swimming around to its other side, I might gain its deck before he knew what had happened.

Somehow, I made it. I broke surface weak and panting but the barge rocked up and down gently—several yards closer to shore. I paddled toward it, hardly using more than my hands, conserving strength, regaining my breath.

No more than four feet off the surface of the water, the deck waited invitingly. I reached the hull, found no hand-hold. Four feet...

I swam along the side of the barge, found halfway to the stern what might have been an anchor chain. Grasping it, I pulled myself out of the water, clambered up and stood dripping on the deck.

ELLEN saw me first and whimpered a little, but Suuki stared at me a moment later—and didn't make a sound. And as I had expected, Ig Karnjud stood at the other side of the craft his back turned, peering out over the water. At that moment the Martians on shore must have spotted me, for they commenced shouting and screaming. Too many of them tried to cry instructions at once, and I don't think Ig Karnjud understood until the very end.

He turned to face me and from somewhere a knife appeared in his hand. He lunged wildly, but I parried the blow with my forearm, felt the knife rip through my jacket-sleeve. Then I hit him. Once and once only, but my right fist caught the point of his chin and threw him bolt upright. He stood there, waving his arms wildly, and then he fell over backwards, hitting the water with a splash.

He screamed, churning the lake into white froth with his arms and legs. Like most Martians, he could not swim—and perhaps that is why these ceremonies were conducted on a barge. Mighty impressive, preaching from the middle of a lake, on a planet where swimming was a rarity and water an awesome spectacle.

Karnjud went down once—and again. I guess I could have gone over the side and hauled him in, but some of the Martians on shore were firing their blasters dangerously close, and I could do nothing but watch the currents carry Ig Karnjud away—and under.

"Thank heaven you came, John!" Ellen cried. Reaction must have set in, for she began to whimper. She'd been very close to death, and she knew it.

Suuki smiled grimly. "We are still not out of this, you know. What do you suggest next, John Hastings?"

Wordlessly, I unbound them. Ellen came down from the pole limply and fell into my arms. We stood that way for a moment, and then I sat her down on the deck, rubbing her wrists and ankles to restore circulation, Dour Suuki had fared much better. He swung around the barge almost jauntily, none the worst for wear.

"There is an old trick," he explained. "You tense the muscles when they bind you, and when you relax the ropes are not particularly oppressive. But what now?"

"Hell," I told him, "just start this boat going, that's all. Right back to where it came from."

"Yes? How?"

"What he means," Ellen told me, "is that there doesn't seem to be any controls. Look for yourself."

I did. A flat barge and nothing more with apparently no way to get down inside.

"Well," I persisted, "how did Karnjud move it?"

Ellen shrugged. "Search me. It just—went."

"Do we stand here and wait for them?" Suuki wanted to know. "In time they will get another boat, you know."

I shook my head. "Can you swim, Suuki?"

He grinned. "You forget, John Hastings, that mine is a watery planet."

"Good. Ellen?"

"A little. No great shakes, John, but a little."

"Suuki, how far would you say this boat came?"

"Merely several hundred yards. There is a dock on the other side of the lake, guarded only by an old caretaker."

"Right. In that case, we'll swim for it."

"What good will that do?" Ellen demanded. "They can follow much faster around the shore—"

"No. You're wrong. They're standing on a little beach, but that's the only shore on this side of the lake. It dips away pretty fast, and sheer rock walls come down to the surface of the water. No one will follow us, Ellen. At least not for a good long while."

Suuki stood poised on the edge of the deck. "In that case, what are we waiting for? They say on my world that a man who delays is—but never mind! Not understanding the language, you'd miss a beautiful play on words. Shall we go?"

Not waiting for an answer, Togoshira Suuki dived overboard. Ellen looked more than a little frightened. Wordless, I took her hand and led her to the side. "Jump," I said. Still holding hands, we leaped.

THE DOCK surprised us. It was an ancient quay jutting out into the lake, but beyond it an underground city loomed in the half-darkness, throwing sword-edged spires up through the phosphorescent murk. Some of the buildings must have been constructed from obsolete spaceship hulls, for they stood poised on their tail-tubes now, seemingly ready to blast-off toward the high-vaulted ceiling of the cavern.

"Apparently religion is a big business with the Martian League," Suuki observed matter-of-factly.

"This kind of religion never did anyone any good," Ellen told him. After that, there wasn't much time for talking. A narrow stone roadway snaked around the edge of the city on a six-foot ledge of what looked like sandstone, and I let Ellen and Suuki use my back as a stepladder to reach it. I caught on with my hands and clambered up after them. Where my hands groped in the gloom, I found a coil of thin but tough rope, and slung it across my arm on the hunch that it might come in handy later. Funny how such hunches can sometimes payoff.

Then, quite suddenly, it began to grow cold. A chill wind swept in off the lake, and that wasn't so bad in itself. But we still wore our drenched garments, and I could tell when I took Ellen's hand in mine that she was shivering.

"Strip," I said.

"What?" Ellen's voice was almost a shriek. I could hear Suuki's dry laughter as he complied.

"Strip," I told Ellen again. "You'll feel warmer if you do." And, when she just stood there I said, "That's an order."

I turned away and peeled off my own wet clothing, then faced them once more. Ellen's skin gleamed wetly in the half-light, and Suuki laughed his dry laugh once more when she tried—and failed—to cover herself with her arms. Suuki pounded his ancient, withered flanks with delight.

When the voice boomed up at us, it sounded like the crack of doom in the utter stillness. "Halt! What was that? *Skarda! Key simlot!*" The guard was bilingual, issuing his order in both English and Martian.

He came into view soon afterwards, a big, hulking half-breed in a fancy dress uniform that must have signified

Martian League soldiery. They had quite an organization, all right. The guard carried a blasting rifle and stood with his feet planted wide right below our position on the ledge.

"Is anyone up there? *Slok kor tini mot?*"

He began to turn slowly as Suuki faded back silently into the shadows. I stood there with Ellen. Both of us naked, unarmed—and helpless. Unarmed? It was almost at the last instant that I remembered my coil of rope.

I EASED it off my shoulder, looped it. I'd have one chance, no more. A blast from the rifle would disembowel me if I didn't cast straight.

I let the rope fly.

Ellen gave a little yelp as it landed on the big man's shoulders. Then I tugged, felt the rope tighten, saw it climb up his neck as I pulled, and fasten just below his chin. I twisted.

His face came half-around in the murk, and I could tell he was trying to scream. No sound escaped his lips. When I let the rope go, the guard slumped to the sandstone, his hands still clawing feebly at his neck.

Then we were running along the ledge without looking back. Finally, we came to a hoary staircase old as the sandstone itself—a twisting staircase that spiraled up dizzily until it disappeared above our heads. A little hut stood at its foot, and this I entered cautiously. Someone inside snored deeply and steadily, and I didn't disturb him. But I came out again with enough evil-smelling Martian clothing for the three of us.

The stairs seemed interminable. We took the garments with us and dressed on the first landing, where Ellen told me my knees were knobby for a Jovian StrongMan. I began an objective discussion of various points of her anatomy, but stopped when she threatened mayhem. She somehow extracted a promise from me not to mention our nakedness together again. Not unless…well, not unless I could remember some of the things John Hastings would have remembered. I nodded quick assent. I'd heard enough about this particular angle of John Hastings' past to want a change of subject—and fast.

From the top of the spiral stairway, a sloping passage led to the surface, and we soon found ourselves on the outskirts of Lake of the Sun City. A bitter night wind whipped in off the desert, bringing flurries of sand with it.

"Venus is such a pleasant place," Suuki muttered. "Even your Earth has its advantages. But this barren mess of a planet—bah!"

We could have remained in the caverns until the sun came up and warmed the desert, but the Martians would not have remained idle. When I told my companions that, Ellen said: "Granted. They'd have us surrounded by morning. Still, we won't get very far in this cold. *Brrr!*" She shivered as a particularly icy blast of wind hit us.

"We don't have to," I told her. "I parked a jet-sled outside the city, maybe a mile from here. I don't know if we can find it in the darkness. We can try…"

And we stalked out into the desert.

PROBABLY Suuki fared the worst. Accustomed to a tropical jungle with tepid waters and steaming swamps, he found himself out on the sub-zero barrens with nothing but a cloak and a cowl to keep out the frigid winds. And the abrupt change in temperature from day to night whipped up a series of never-diminishing sandstorms, driving tiny pellets against us with almost hurricane force.

After a time, it became a blinding, stinging nightmare. It was an effort even to pick up your feet and push them forward for the next step. I grew numb all over, not slowly, but within moments after we had set out. The winds howled, the sands whirled high in furious little eddies, which blotted out the stars.

We trudged on half a mile, maybe three-quarters—and then Suuki collapsed. I could barely make out Ellen's face in the darkness, but I could see that she looked down at him helplessly.

"We can't leave him," she said. "He'll die. But we can't stay on here. John—Johnny, I'm frightened."

Suuki gasped, "Go—ahead. Foolish—to stay. A shame...John Hastings...for there is so...much we could have—told each—other!"

I smiled. "Will you still feel like talking if we can get back to Syrtis?"

He grunted an answer, but it was lost in the shrilling winds. I lifted him off the sands, slung him over my shoulder. Here on Mars with its lighter gravity he didn't carry much more than half his real weight, and I plodded on, letting StrongMan Bok-kura do the rest.

Ellen grasped my free hand with her own stiff fingers, and walking that way we reached the jet-sled—parked near a monument that proclaimed Lake of the Sun City to be a peaceful old settlement, which reminded one of the old days of Mars, with boats floating serenely down the canals, men and maids carousing in the warm sunshine, and nothing more than an occasional gust of balmy wind to stir the tranquil scene...

CHAPTER FIVE
Fat Man Asteroid

"HOW DO you do?" Dr. Elkins said. "So you're Togoshira Suuki, the famous Venusian asteroidologist."

Suuki smiled. "I'd be nothing at all if Hastings hadn't carried me off the desert two nights ago. I think I am very glad the man was my hobby."

I laughed. "Be gladder still that I played a Jovian Strong Man for a couple of years. You don't weigh as much as those barbells, Suuki."

"So *that's* where you disappeared! How did it come about?"

"I don't remember—remember?"

"He's stubborn," Dr. Elkins said. "If he'd submit to treatment, we might have his memory back inside of six months."

"I'd like that," Ellen admitted. I held her hand and, warm now, her fingers were pleasant to touch.

"The answer is still no, doc. I got what I came to Mars for—Suuki here. There's a lot he can tell me, so if you think he's well enough—"

"Certainly he's well. The cold sapped his strength, but the man's heart is as strong as a machine. Don't worry about that." And Dr. Elkins put away his stethoscope confidently.

Suuki sat up in bed, smoothing the covers over his scrawny chest. "About three years ago," the uplander-Jap began, "the whole solar system waited breathlessly for word from you. You'd discovered an asteroid that allegedly contained artifacts of a culture that existed before a planet between Mars and Jupiter exploded.

"Your last message to North American University was optimistic. You'd uncovered the artifacts, all right. Now, all you had to do was interpret them. But you were never heard from again...

"Months later, they found your ship, a derelict, floating free outside the asteroid swarm. No John Hastings. No written records. Nothing. But plenty of food, air, and water. You met with an accident, it was assumed. And obviously, you'd met death out there on some uncharted asteroid. Expeditions set out to find you but came back empty-handed. John Hastings was forgotten.

"But the mystery of the asteroids wasn't. The old Martian civilization somehow connects its myths of the asteroids with a doctrine of eternal life. And rumors spread. You'd found that, John Hastings—the secret of regeneration, of eternal life—and you'd perished with it. Is it any wonder that people sought you?

"Earth-government scoffed mightily at the whole idea, but the navy maintains a carefully guarded operation, Project H. H for Hastings! Venus and Mars have their underground agents at work, too, and the Sargasso Cities hold the spotlight, because government men can work outside the law there, without the necessity of reporting back officially. Venus wants the secret—hence the upland Brotherhood, with some Earth members too, since some of your planeteers feel that the Brotherhood can put the secret to better use. Mars wants it—hence the League. And Earth is also determined to get it."

"When I came to Mars," I said, "someone tried to kill me. How can you explain that?"

Suuki shrugged eloquently enough. "Sargasso City. Intrigue and counter intrigue. News of your arrival came to Mars before you did."

"And one of your agents in Lake of the Sun City—a woman named Beta something—turned out to be in cahoots with the League."

"The same. It's difficult to maintain vigil over an underground organization that covers three planets and the Jovian moons as well."

"ALL RIGHT, answer this one. Before I knew what was going on, a man on Earth tried to kill me. He was injured— severely. And walked away a few minutes later."

"Regeneration," Suuki mused. "How else can I explain it? Does it mean the rumors are true?"

"It does," Dr. Elkins said. He told Suuki how they'd found me out on the desert.

I shook my head. "That isn't what I'm getting at. A man tried to kill me, almost succeeded. But where did he fit into the picture? How did he know me back there at the sideshow when no one else did? Remember, Suuki, at the time you didn't know I was alive. We can assume the same for the Martian League. But some other force knew, found me and wanted me dead. But why? The Martians tried to kill me so I couldn't reach you. I guess they were afraid of what we could do about this regeneration stuff if we ever got together. But otherwise, the Marties would have wanted me alive. The same goes for your Brotherhood. What I want to know is this: why did that someone else want me dead?"

"What you're asking," Dr. Elkins said, "is something like this: one particular party, and one only, did not want you alive. A dead John Hastings couldn't return to the asteroids, let alone lead a new scientific expedition out there. Thus, someone wished to put a stop to the whole thing." He frowned. "I can't make anything out of that part of it either."

Ellen spoke for the first time. "Maybe I can," she said. "We'd been in radio contact almost to the end, Johnny. Every day you got more excited, I remember it almost like it was yesterday. But you couldn't tell me anything concrete, not really concrete, because you feared someone else might cut in on the frequency, and what you'd found was dynamite. Also," she blushed a little, "you were kept much too busy telling me how much you loved me..."

I felt like a damned fool, for I remembered nothing. It isn't easy, people telling you what you did, what you said and everything is an absolute blank to you. I cleared my throat self-consciously and told Ellen to continue.

"WELL, YOU spoke about that old Martian myth, regeneration of tissues. I think, above all, that you wanted to impress upon me the fact that it wasn't so far-fetched. 'Look,' you said, 'a man gets a cut, it heals. An abrasion too, but sometimes there's a scar. A broken bone will knit. But that's only half the story. Plants regenerate their tissues all the time. Did you know that a plant doesn't really stop growing until it ceases to live? Or take some of the more primitive animals. On Earth, cut an arm off a starfish and it will grow a new one. Same for a lobster and its claws and, to a lesser extent, for the insects. Same on Mars, and it holds true to an even greater extent among the primitive life forms of Venus. There's nothing odd about it, nothing smacking of the supernatural. It's nature's way of protecting some of its species, and there's no reason to believe that advanced science couldn't extend regeneration to man as well.

" 'I'll be able to prove that soon,' you said. 'And don't be surprised if I bring the proof back in a mighty shocking form. Tell me, kid, would you be willing to marry a superman?' " Ellen crimsoned slightly. "Oh, maybe those weren't the exact words, but you said something like that. I never heard from you again."

Suuki smiled grimly. "It all points to one thing. John, you must find that asteroid again…"

"Sure," I said, "just like that. One asteroid out of ten thousand, only I can't remember which one."

"It is not impossible. First, you must return to the asteroid belt—and then let's see if your memory can't pick up the lost threads. I believe—"

"By George!" Dr. Elkins cried. "What a glorious challenge. The power to change mankind at your fingertips, if only you could remember. I will go along."

I told Suuki, "All I want to know is this: how are we going to get there?"

"My friend, the Brotherhood is not without its power, even here in Syrtis. We can raise the money; with it we can buy a ship; and then we'll see."

Dr. Elkins grabbed his hand impulsively. "Suuki, if this works out, science will remember you as a great man."

The uplander-Jap chuckled dryly. "I'm far more interested in the Brotherhood."

"I only want Johnny to regain his memory," Ellen said.

And that seemed to be that. Each of them had his reason for wanting to reach the asteroids with me in tow. Well, I had my reasons too, but somehow—as Suuki began to make preparations—a cold chill crept over me. Between Mars and Jupiter, there was a broad sector of space which, according to the famous law of Bode, should have been the orbit for a great planet. Instead, the thousands of asteroids spun out there in their cold dead vault, mute remains of a planet that existed—how many millions of years ago? And something out there had taken my memory from me, had given in its place something nameless, something that branded me for all the worlds to see: *This man is more than human!*

Was that something still lurking out in the cold bleak marches of space?

MARS FADED behind us, a swollen ochre and crimson globe. Ahead, the tiny motes that were asteroids caught the sunlight, held it, threw it back at us—a thousand or more points of light. The rockets of Suuki's battered, secondhand cruiser throbbed dully from somewhere deep in the bowels of the ship. Elkins was asleep now, and Suuki. I stood with Ellen in the control chamber, plotting an aimless course.

"Where will we go?" she wanted to know.

"Search me. Suuki thinks it ought to be haphazard at first. Maybe something will strike a familiar chord for me."

"I hope so, Johnny. I hope so."

Mars-light flooded in through the huge quartzite windows, suffusing everything with a delicate saffron glow. Deep space encroached on all sides trying, it almost seemed, to force its way in through the windows, through the observation dome overhead, through the ports with their translucent coverings. But there was something of comfort within the ship, of security, of that unnamed thing that through the ages has permitted mankind to thumb its nose at the perils of a hostile environment.

I didn't know what at first. I suppose it's different for every man, for each his own private, inviolate sanctuary. And mine?

Ellen came to me slowly, the saffron highlights gleaming in her hair. Her eyes were big and wide and pleading. They said, *remember, Johnny! Oh, can't you please remember?*

She brushed against my chest, the faintest suggestion of a touch, and then I'd folded my arms around her, pulled her in close, felt the arch of her back grow stiff for a moment, then relax. I touched her hair with my lips, her brow, her eyes, the smooth supple curve of her neck...

A small voice, almost that of a child: "Johnny, Johnny—you remember!"

I kissed the words from her lips, softly at first. I held it a long time, that kiss, not softly any longer. Toward the end it must have hurt her.

For Ellen, a ghost from the past, phantom no more. For me, the first sweet-brutal kiss of new love. "Johnny, you *do* remember!"

"Do you mind terribly if I don't?"

"I—I don't understand you."

"I remember nothing, not now, not yet. I only know that suddenly I had to do that. Not to remember anything, Ellen, but just for now, for today—and—"

"And what, Johnny?"

"And for tomorrow, too. Ellen—you hear it so much, you read it in books, but then when you try to say it yourself, it doesn't sound right. It sounds corny. It—hell, I don't care! Ellen, I—I think I'm falling in love with you. No, wait. Not the old John Hastings who everyone wants to remember. But me, right now, today. *I* love you, Ellen. I love you!"

"Johnny—"

It couldn't last. Something had to break the spell. An instant later I plummeted from the heights to the depths—and it looked as if I'd stay there for a long time. Maybe permanently.

The two remaining brothers Karnjud stood in the doorway, blasters in their hands.

"SIT RIGHT there," the English-speaking brother said. "Don't move. Don't make a sound. I'm warning you."

Ellen whispered, "I know them! Their brother took me, that Ig Karnjud…"

They stalked into the control room, grim as pallbearers. Maybe they'd heard of their brother's death, maybe they'd somehow gotten wind of our expedition, hidden themselves aboard the ship. I didn't know, not then.

They ignored Ellen, marching forward grimly until they; stood right in front of me.

"You rotten, stinking bastard!" the older brother cried. "You killed Ig—"

He slashed down with the blaster, bringing the tube end down across my cheek, opening it to the bone. I stumbled back, swung wildly with my right hand, but Karnjud side-stepped easily. "Don't try that again, Hastings. My brother will kill you."

He meant it, and all I could do was stand there and take a beating.

He swung the blaster down again, handling it gracefully, more like a whip than a gun. It crashed against the bridge of my nose, cut further and ripped my lips. I heard Ellen whimper from far off, dimly saw her throw herself against the Martian. He muttered an oath, hurled her off into a corner. She got up again, yelling like a banshee, but the other Karnjud clipped her jaw with his fist and she tumbled over backwards, falling in a heap on the floor.

"Damn it, leave her out of this! Yeah, I killed your brother, but she had nothing to do with it."

"Ain't that lovely. He wants to protect her..."

The blaster slammed down once more, crashing against my temple, stunning me. I stumbled, slumped half-forward, felt something explode against the back of my neck. It sent me all the way down to the floor, and I hit hard.

I had time to roll over on my back, to hunch up and tense my muscles. By then, the older Karnjud had forgotten all about his blaster. I saw him leering down at me through a bloody haze, saw his brother's blaster, unwavering, pointing at me.

A foot lashed out and I tried to ride with it, but it caught me down near the kidneys, I think, and a wave of agony washed over me. Again, higher up this time, digging into the ribs. Still higher, numbing my shoulder. When the heavy boot started for my face, I was drifting away on a sea of crimson fog. The boot seemed to hang suspended in that fog, but it stalked me...

Far away, Suuki's voice: "What's the meaning of—"

Then the boot struck.

"GET UP!" Something prodded my face, urgently.

"On your feet, Hastings. Come on. The way your body can regenerate injured tissue, you're not hurt."

As a matter of fact, I wasn't. I hadn't been unconscious for long, but it had been sufficient time for me to heal. Wipe the blood away, and I'd look like new. I felt it, too. Almost chipper. Hell, let them do what they want, they couldn't hurt me, not really.

Them!

The first voice belonged to Karnjud. The second was Dr. Elkin's!

I stood up fast, the Karnjuds waving me off into a corner with their blasters. Mars had faded behind us and the ship's pale blue spacelights cast harsh shadows across Dr. Elkins' mild face. He smiled coldly. "I suppose you are surprised, Hastings."

"You're damned right I'm surprised!"

"You needn't be. The Martie who attempted to take your life out on the desert was a member of an extremist group. I am not an extremist although, frankly, I was hard put to keep the Karnjuds off you after what happened to their brother. I merely work through the Martian League in the interests of science—as I can apply it. What is science, Hastings, unless one can apply it, twist it for his own purposes, mold it to make a better world for himself?

"We want you alive. We want you to find that asteroid for us. Unfortunately, your friend Togoshira Suuki desires the same thing, but the Brotherhood claims an altruistic motive. I put it up to you, Hastings: altruistic, bah! In science one learns that there is no such thing. Each creature, each species, functions only in terms of its own survival. If something has survival value, it is good. If it does not, it is evil. Do I make myself clear?"

"Damned clear," I said. Mild-mannered Dr. Elkins, an egocentric creature who hid his self-importance behind a garb of modest scientific endeavor. But I knew he could be the most dangerous sort of antagonist, for he believed in his own warped creed.

"Where's Suuki?" I asked him. I think I was a little afraid to ask about Ellen.

"He's well, don't worry. And the girl, too. Suuki has knowledge that may aid us, and the girl might possibly help you remember. For now, Hastings, they have survival value. Don't misunderstand me, I hold no hatred for you. I believe I said I was intrigued once, and I meant that. But you have survival value as well...and so I need you. And don't you forget it."

IT DIDN'T help much to think about it now, but I'd been an idiot. Seemingly on a whim, Elkins had given up his Syrtis Major medical practice to come with us on this jaunt through the asteroids. He'd planned it that way all along, which also could explain his original desire to help me regain my memory. Scientific interest, sure—but directed toward his own ends.

"You've got the deck stacked all the way," I told him. "How's it going to be dealt, Doc?"

"You'll see in a few hours, Hastings. We're nearing the asteroid belt now, and there is an advanced base that our organization holds in readiness. According to the Karnjud boys, our leader will be there. Can you believe that I've never met our leader? Strange, for I am the prime cog in our not-very-small machine. Perhaps our leader has other ideas. Perhaps... We'll see.

"Meanwhile, I leave you with the brothers Karnjud. As a word of advice, try nothing foolish. I believe I have impressed upon them the necessity of keeping you alive, but they remember their brother and the Martians are a peculiar people, placing vendetta over survival value. Well, good day." And he walked from the room, still a mild-looking little man.

The place, I realized, was a storeroom, deep within the ship. You had to speak loudly over the insistent *throb-throb-throb* of the rockets. The older Karnjud locked and bolted the heavy metal door, spoke for a time with his brother, in Martian. Then he turned to face me.

"Luka thinks I ain't treating him right. He says I knocked hell outa you before, he didn't. He wants to do it now. You know what, Hastings? I think I'm gonna let him. No, stay back! Just get off in that corner. That's right. I'm standing right here, see, and don't you forget it. My brother Luka is gonna wade into you till he gets tired. If you so much as raise a finger, I'll kill you."

Grinning inanely, Luka shuffled forward, somewhat on the tall side and incredibly thin, even for a Martian. I don't think he weighed a hundred pounds, but I had a hunch he'd know how to wield the butt of a blaster.

I didn't wait to find out.

HIS BROTHER wasn't kidding, he'd gun me down if I tried anything. Only what he did not realize was this—Luka stood between us.

Luka raised the blaster in his thin fingers and brought it down. I moved in quick, caught his wrist and turned it. He howled once, then fell in toward me. I spun him around, got one hand on the back of his belt, one on the collar of his shirt. He came up off the floor easily, and I hurled him at his brother.

Karnjud fired his blaster instinctively, its beam searing Luka. His howl became a gurgle that bubbled from his throat. His chest and stomach scorched to a blackened ruin, Luka was dead before he hit the floor.

Karnjud knew it without bothering to look. He whimpered frightfully, an animal sound. He fired again, but by then I'd ducked behind a packing crate which the beam kindled to quick flame. I got away fast, but Karnjud hardly seemed aware of the fire licking up at us. "Luka," he mumbled over and over again. "Luka, Luka, Luka…"

He hardly saw me. He criss-crossed the room with raw energy, bringing angry flames wherever the beam touched. Smoke made it difficult to breathe—and to see. Karnjud stood at the bolted door, firing his blaster and screaming, firing and screaming.

Somehow, I got to him, took the blaster from his fingers, pushed him aside. I turned my attention to the door, reaching out for the bolt and then drawing my hands away. The door was red-hot!

Gibbering now, Karnjud sat down near his dead brother, near the brother he'd killed with his own hand. "Luka, Luka! Say you're not dead! Luka, speak to me. Luka—"

I tried to drag him away, but he kicked out at me, scurried like some midnight rodent to the other side of Luka's corpse and stayed there. He sat that way, a ring of flame closing around him, and I couldn't argue, not unless I wanted to become a part of it.

I ripped a strip of cloth from my sleeve, bound it around my right hand. With this I tackled the scorching bolt and soon I'd thrown it back, opening the door. I looked once more into the storeroom, now a roaring, raging inferno. Of the dead Luka and his brother I could see nothing.

Outside, I shut the door, gulped in great lung fulls of fresh air. Then I ran forward.

Suuki and Ellen sat in the control room, bound to two of the pilot seats. Dr. Elkins was busy at the controls.

"Close off aft!" I cried. "Fire!"

"Fire?" Elkins snorted.

"Damn it, that's what I said."

"This ship is fireproof," he told me blandly.

"The storerooms aren't. Karnjud is back there with his brother, dead. The whole place is one roaring mess of flames!"

Smoke drifted into the control room, and Elkins jumped to his feet. "What section?"

"Four," I told him.

"Well, we'll shut it off. This ship is compartmented, no harm will be done. The fire will burn itself out, leave a hole in the hull. But we have nothing to worry about."

"That's what you think. Section four lies adjacent to the engine room. The heat's liable to fuse the softer metals down there and turn us into a derelict."

FOR THE first time, Elkins appeared alarmed. "Wh— what do you want me to do?"

"Like you said, shut off section four. Then we'll have to high tail it for the nearest asteroid. I hope we make it!"

Elkins pressed a stud, and from somewhere back in the rear of the ship, great metal doors clanged shut. "The nearest asteroid is our advanced base, Hastings. But will we make it? My God, will we make it?"

"Survival value doesn't look so hot now, huh, Doc? I don't know, how long will it take?"

"Umm-mm. Another hour at top speed. I don't know if we can stand the acceleration."

I told him we'd have to, but when he made no move to throw the rocket levers all the way home, I thrust him away from the control board and sat down there myself.

He'd forgotten all about the blaster in his hand. "I don't want to die," he said. "Not burning up like this in space. I have so much to do."

Full-rockets jarred me, squeezing me back into my chair. I heard Ellen whimper, saw Suuki's acceleration-distorted face. Elkins had fainted at the first new thrust.

The pressure was bad enough, but with it came heat, burning, blinding heat. I stuck grimly with the controls, but I began to feel we'd never make it. Then I heard Ellen trying to say something.

"Sil-ly. Don't shut…off section…four! Open it—to - space…instead. No oxygen…to burn—with!"

Of course! Neither Elkins nor I had thought of that, but it was the obvious thing to do. Open a porthole in section four, let all the air *woosh* out, and you'd have no more fire.

I pushed the rocket-lever back to the right, felt acceleration ease off gradually. Then I stood up, crossed to the repair cabinet, took out a spacesuit. Made to withstand all extremes of temperature, it could take me safely through the roaring flames of section four.

The rest was easy. Wearing the spacesuit, I ran back through the companionway, worked the manual levers on the compartment doors, entered the cauldron of fire that was section four. Once and once only I struck out at one of the ports with a gauntleted fist. I watched the quartzite shatter and fly out into the vacuum of space. Air rushed out after it, sucked from an area of pressure to one that lacked it altogether. When I looked again into the storeroom, the fire had vanished. Utterly, as if it had never been. Smoke had rushed with the air through the port, flames had subsided instantly with no oxygen left to support combustion.

Charred, blackened horrors where the Karnjud brothers had lain…

I got out of my spacesuit in the companionway, marched up to the control room with it slung over my arm. Elkins was waiting for me, and this time he did not forget his blaster. He held it firmly and it pointed at my chest and he said: "Come in and sit down. I can be wrong about survival value, Hastings. Don't try me."

Maybe he'd counted on the brothers Karnjud for some support when he met the unknown leader. I could sense something there, something that might help us later. Without knowing him, Dr. Elkins hated this man who presided over intrigue on three worlds, who held the whip hand in a game that Elkins wanted completely for his own.

Wearily, I sat near Ellen, smiled into her eyes. She looked tired, but she smiled back.

Suuki was sound asleep.

I ASKED Elkins' permission to release Ellen from her bonds. He granted it readily enough, but refused to offer the same freedom to the sleeping Suuki.

Ellen whispered, "It all happened so fast before, you didn't have time to finish what you were saying, did you?"

"No," I told her. "You're wrong. I said all I wanted to say. No strings attached, kid. I love you."

"Then you must remember! Surely you must remember something."

"I only wish I did. But no, it isn't like that at all. I fell in love with you, and it's still as if the old John Hastings never existed. Hell, I don't know. Maybe a part of my mind that can't understand remembered. But only you, Ellen, and how I feel about you. Everything else is a complete blank."

She pouted. "What I don't understand is that your body can regenerate itself, right?

I'd nodded.

"Well, how about your mind, your memory? Why can't that do the same thing?"

"Don't look at me. I haven't got the slightest idea how this thing works. So—since I don't remember—I guess it doesn't include that."

We rambled on and on, about everything, about nothing. We lost all track of time. It came pretty much as a surprise when I heard Elkins talking excitedly into the radio.

"Yes, that's what I said. We're with the League. I have Togoshira Suuki on board, a prisoner. Right. I suppose that does take the sting out of the Upland Brotherhood. And I have another surprise for you. John Hastings is on this ship, also a prisoner. I am Dr. Ronald Elkins—ah, you know of me! Unfortunately, I can't say the same concerning you. What? Yes, I suppose I will see you in a few minutes. Will I know you? Umm, you don't think so, eh? Well, I can't help being curious."

THROUGH the observation dome, I could see a great slab of rock tumbling along through the void. That's one thing you can't get used to about the asteroids. All of them aren't round. Oh, there are mathematical laws that insist that the larger ones, like Ceres and Vesta, assume spherical form, but some of the smaller baby planets can come in the damndest shapes. Twisting end over and several miles in space, headquarters for the Martian League looked a lot like a pockmarked coffin.

"I suppose you don't know your astronomy," Elkins commented smugly. "That planetoid is Eros, twenty miles or so in diameter. And look...look there! See that shining thing? The league built a pressure dome there! It will be just like home under it, unless the leader happens to be a Martian. Then it will be just like Mars."

"Did he sound like a Martian?" I asked.

"No. No, he didn't. Earthman, I'd say. But I've never heard his voice before—that's a certainty. I wonder who he is."

Well, I was wondering the same thing, too. And I had an odd hunch that I'd know the man. Nothing I could put my finger on, but it kept insisting, that hunch—and it said, plainly enough, *you'll be in for a surprise.*

We landed some three or four hundred yards from the huge quartzite dome, and Eros was a weird place. Pock-marked and scarred like the surface of the moon, covered with a powdery, virgin-white pumice, it stretched out unevenly in all directions. Off to the left, the horizon jutted up in a wild profusion of rocky crags not more than a hundred yards away. Twenty miles long, Eros was no more than two or three miles wide, and we stood near one edge of its rectangular surface. Straight ahead, however, we could see for miles, except where the quartzite rose out of the pumice and obstructed our view.

ELKINS watching us carefully, we climbed into our spacesuits, set our gravity equalizers, stepped out on the surface of Eros. In a matter of minutes we reached the dome, shuffled forward into an airlock, waited till a red light blinked on and off telling us that pressure and atmosphere had been built up within the lock. We took off our spacesuits, hung them along with many others on the pegs that lined one wall. Then we walked through the inner door and inside the dome.

It was very pleasant inside—about Earth temperature, perhaps sixty-five degrees. And a delicious fragrance of growing green things, which was like heaven after the parched air of Mars and the canned air of a spaceship.

Half a dozen Marties met us, uncomfortable in what was to them a thick, soupy atmosphere. Apparently Elkins knew the Martie in charge, for some civil words passed between them. They ushered us forward, past a row of hastily constructed barracks, down a wide, tree-shaded lane. Evidently this Earthman leader of the League liked his terrestrial comforts!

The big house at the end of the street did not show signs of hasty construction. It had been done carefully, painstakingly, a big sprawling structure of some nameless white stone. At the entrance, a Martian houseboy met us and told us to wait. He returned in a moment and said, "My masser see you now. Please to wipe feet if dirty."

How prissy could you get on a flyspeck of a frontier world!

The leader of the Martian League sat at his desk in a large study. His back was turned to us, a huge back, very wide and very fleshy. Sweat stained the back of his gray shirt a darker color, despite the pleasant temperature. I could just see the side of his jaw, and it worked up and down, up and down. He chewed noisily, his fat arm rising and falling into a bowl of fruit. I couldn't be sure, because we only saw his back from where we stood—but I'd have bet he weighed close to five hundred pounds.

He turned slowly, indolently—and faced us. I let out an audible gasp, and I suddenly felt weak. Dr. Elkins' place in the Martian League order of things had come as a distinct shock. This was worse.

Sweat streaming down his face as he swiveled around in his chair, fruit juices staining the corners of his blubbery lips, the leader of the Martian League chuckled softly. He was Lope Perez, the Fat Man of Venezuela!

CHAPTER SIX
Perez's Story

"SURPRISED, Bok-kura? Or should I say John Hastings?" The same syrupy voice that I remembered so well. How long ago had it been? "No, I guess it will remain Bok-kura, eh, Boky? Well, say something! Don't just stand there like an idiot. Ahh, these synthetic nectarines are good!"

I mumbled a word or two about not understanding, and Perez snorted, "Bah! I can believe that. Give a man a sound body and he'll forget all about his mind, permit it to atrophy. But make him too big or too small or malformed in some other way, and he'll have to use his brain. You're a fool, Boky..."

Dr. Elkins shook his head. "I don't agree," he said. "The mind and the body work together as one. The best combination offers the best possible survival value."

Perez snorted once more. "And just who the hell are you, my little popinjay?"

"Elkins. I radioed—"

"Ah, yes. Elkins. Will you be good enough to shut your mouth and let me talk?"

This wasn't the Perez I had known, not the weak, sniveling mountain of a man. Oh, the flesh was there, and the propensity for sweating, and the appetite. But Lope Perez had played a different role entirely in Dufree's sideshow, and I told him that.

He said, "Don't you think I'm aware of it? Don't you think I hated every moment of it? Parading around for the gawking hicks who came to watch, taking orders from everyone in the company, living in filth? Bah! Many times I thought I should have to quit, but I always saw you there, Boky, and so I remained.

"PERHAPS you wonder why I helped you that last day, perhaps you wonder about that and a lot more. It was a long haul and a thankless one, but that day I knew you were on your way. You had to go free, don't you understand? If the police took you, if they allowed Dufree's trumped-up charge to stick, you might still be in prison. But you escaped, and things began falling neatly into place after that.

"I found you at the Spaceport long ago. *I* found you, not Dufree. You hadn't forgotten everything yet, but your memory was fading fast. You told me many things. And then you lost consciousness. When you came to, you remembered nothing. But you'd said enough to whet my appetite, Boky. I had to find out the rest. I knew of John Hastings, almost everyone did. If you lived too public a life after that I knew the government would find you, and that would be the end for Perez.

"On the other hand, there would be nothing to trigger your memory if you lived in seclusion. Dufree's sideshow was the middle of the road. Someone might recognize you, yes—but I could act before official circles. And that is precisely what happened. You became the strong man, me...I was the fat clown. No, I don't begrudge the fat part of it, Boky. If a man loves food inordinately he will grow obese. It is the price he has to pay"—munching on another juicy piece of fruit—"and I say it is worth it. But I played the buffoon. I, Perez, played the buffoon, and that I did not like..."

"Want to keep talking?" I said. "I hope so, because I'm still all mixed up."

"Why not? If I expect you to help me I suppose you must learn at least part of the truth. You landed on Earth with another man, with a freight captain who'd found you out here in the asteroids. Evidently he shared in your secrets, for he too had the powers of regeneration. He tried to kill you that last day at Dufree's. Ah, you remember? The way I connect things, it happened like this: somehow, you lost your ship out here. You were stranded on an asteroid, and by a thousand-to-one chance that man found you, shared in your secret, took you back to Earth. Apparently he wanted to exploit what you'd found, you did not. A fight ensued, and somehow he won. Perhaps by trickery. At any rate, you received a nasty bang on the head, and amnesia resulted.

"The other man escaped. When he found you by chance that day at Dufree's, he did not know you had lost your memory. He was determined to kill you, to keep the secret for himself. How could he expect to kill you knowing that you shared with him the powers of regeneration? I don't know. Maybe he acted foolishly in spite of it. Although I rather suspect the power has its Achilles' Heel. Perhaps the needle gun he tried to use, perhaps something else. All I know for sure is this—that man is now dead, and he had this power of yours."

"Dead?"

"Yes. I went looking for him, figuring he could answer everything you could. I found him, and he ran. We had him trapped in a farmhouse, we fired the house to force his surrender. He got caught, couldn't extricate himself. When the fire burned itself out, he was dead—burned to a crisp—and there was nothing left to regenerate. So you see, Bok-kura, you are not invulnerable. I would suggest you remember that."

SUUKI JOINED the conversation for the first time. "Then there yet remains one thing—"

"Umm-mm, you'd be this Brotherhood, Upland-hood, whatever it is—you'd be their leader, Togoshira Suuki. You realize, of course, Mr. Suuki, that the span of your life is limited precisely by what aid you can offer me. As the expression has it, we play on opposite teams."

Suuki chose to ignore the threat. "As I have said, one thing remains. We have not yet located the asteroid on which all this happened."

"No?" Perez smiled. "Perhaps your Brotherhood hasn't. We of the League have. Our archaeologists have been able to make nothing out of it, I am ashamed to admit. All they know is that they have found the seat of a very ancient civilization. Better minds than theirs are needed."

"Suuki," I said. "You'll need Suuki."

"Wrong. We'll need *you*. Your friend will have to prove his worth in some other way if he desires life instead of death."

"No, you're wrong. I forget all my technical training. I didn't even know I was an archaeologist until someone told me. You'll need Suuki, like I said."

"Don't dictate to me! I'll—well, we'll see. Further, what do you suppose I'm going to do with the girl?"

I took an angry stride toward the Fat Man, but Elkins waved me away with his blaster. Suuki said. "You will do absolutely nothing with Miss Crewson. Otherwise, we won't lift a finger to help you. You find your hands tied, do you not?"

"Forget it, Suuki," I said. "All we can do is wait for something to happen."

Suuki nodded slowly. "I suppose you are right, my friend. He can leave all of us on an airless little coffin of a world after we do his work for him."

I DIDN'T say anything. Suuki was right, of course. But I knew that I'd kill Perez if he as much as touched Ellen.

"...so," Perez was saying, "that leaves absolutely nothing. After this ability to regenerate is in my hands, nothing will stop me. Do you realize what it will mean? The old will come to me, the crippled, the feeble. Everyone. They'll pay anything, they'll sign their lives away for a touch of it."

Dr. Elkins shouted, "No! No, that's all wrong! That's not the way *I* planned it."

"You? And who do you think you are? Do you think you count?"

"I have plans," Elkins persisted. "Selfish plans, yes—but I insist that we go about this more slowly, experimenting, determining just what this regeneration can do and what it cannot. Perhaps after ten years—"

"Ten years! You're insane. I'll control the Three Worlds inside of a year!"

"In that case, you'll do it without me."

There Elkins made his mistake. Somehow, he felt he was important, felt in some obscure way that the whole business could not proceed without him.

Perez began to laugh, the fat under his chin wagging from side to side, jiggling up and down. "You are quite sure, Dr. Elkins?"

"Of course I'm sure."

"You won't change your mind?"

Elkins had not seen it, but Perez's fat hand had crept to a button on his desk. Three Marties came into the room, soundlessly. They stood behind the bald doctor and they waited.

Perez said, "You will take this man outside the dome and kill him." He munched on another nectarine, smiling when Elkins began to lift his blaster. He never got it all the way up. Strong hands pinned his arms from behind, lifted him off the floor, bore him away. He didn't begin to scream until they had shut the door quietly behind them.

"NOW THEN," Perez told us, "we will leave for your asteroid tomorrow, Boky. You, me, Suuki here, the girl. I suggest you all get a good night's sleep."

"What happens afterwards?"

"Boky! Boky, don't you trust me?"

"You know damned well I don't."

"It doesn't matter. What happens afterwards is my concern only. For now, will you come here, Boky?"

I walked to his desk and stood there. He reached into a drawer, came up with a knife, which he probably used to pit his fruit. "I've always wanted to see how it works, Boky. Do you mind? There's a good fellow, put your arm on the desk, please."

Ellen began to sob, but I heard Suuki quieting her. I extended my arm, watched while Perez brought his knife close, placed its point just above the large veins on my wrist. With a quick motion, he slashed the knife across my forearm. He'd severed the veins, and blood began to pour out at once. Soon it slowed to a trickle, then stopped altogether. Grunting his satisfaction, Perez wiped it away with a cloth, looked at my arm. A thin white scar—nothing more.

"Wonderful, Boky! Utterly wonderful. Do you realize that with your secret I shall be able to—well, no matter. I am tried and I wish to nap before eating. My men will show you out."

"He's a megalomaniac," Suuki whispered as we left the room. "Did you see that? He knows he needs you, John, but his mind is so tightly wrapped around this regeneration process that he had to see it for himself. Had he underestimated its powers, you might have bled to death."

"I knew nothing would happen."

"Yes, I know! But that fat man—what's his name, Perez? Thank you. Perez did not know. He took a chance, a foolish one. We should keep that in mind. I think that if the opportunity presents itself, we may put that to use."

I nodded, but I wasn't listening. Tomorrow. Tomorrow we'd visit the source of the mystery. I'd found something there once, and I'd almost perished. Perez had been helpful, he'd explained a lot. But I wasn't entirely satisfied, and although I was eager, I also was afraid of what the morrow might bring.

Ellen must have sensed it. She took my hand and squeezed it, and sometimes the way she looked at me she could say "I love you" without uttering a sound.

BEHIND us, Eros tumbled along through the void, a great stone coffin, spinning end over end. Perez sat at the controls, three of his Martians lolled about the control room. I paced back and forth and Suuki paced with me. He said, "I'd have liked to approach this asteroid differently, John. I'd have liked to approach it with the trained archaeologists of the Brotherhood. Now—now we're in the hands of some common thugs, and a madman who wants to use regeneration for his own ends."

I smiled. "Maybe it won't be as bad as all that, Suuki. Perez doesn't know archaeology; sure as hell none of his Marties do. So he needs us. When we get there, well—we'll see."

Perez called triumphantly from his seat: "We're coming! There it is, just ahead. Look if you'd care to, and remember it was, I, Perez, who discovered—"

"*Re*discovered, you mean," Suuki told him. "John Hastings found the place originally, provided you have the right asteroid."

"Oh, it's the right one, don't you worry about that. See for yourself…"

Interested, Suuki crossed to the port, and I saw Ellen get up and follow him. For a while I hung back. I felt all choked up inside, and when Ellen saw I wasn't going to watch with them, she came back for me.

"Hey, don't tell me the man responsible for all this doesn't want to be on hand when—"

"I don't know. Maybe it's not the right place. Maybe it is. Maybe I'm scared…" You couldn't blame me. Without knowing how or why, I'd been made something more than a man at this asteroid which now swam up rapidly in the port. And someone—or something—had left a message in my pocket. *Have caution, John Hastings, they may try to kill you.* Sure, men like Perez would cheerfully kill for the secret of regeneration, but that wasn't it. Who had left the message? And why?

Well, I'd come a long way to find out, and when Ellen walked back to the port I followed on her heels.

IT HOVERED off in space, that asteroid, black as jet. It should have been entirely invisible, for it shed no light at all. But behind it the stars of deep space formed a speckled backdrop and it stood starkly silhouetted against them, darker than the night side of Pluto. At first I couldn't guess its size, but Perez had started deceleration—and that meant we were close. It also meant the asteroid had a maximum diameter of perhaps two or three miles. Utterly black and utterly round.

Artificial?

Perez was fat and he didn't look like much of an astrogator, but he knew how to bring the ship down. We landed with scarcely a bump. The three Marties stood off at one side of the control room, muttering among themselves.

Perez looked at them, snorted. "All right! Don't stand there all day. Get a move on."

"Masser," said one, "old story long before Earthman come talk of small black planet. Much mystery. Much death. No good."

"We're going outside. You're coming with us."

"Masser, Mars men have much fear. We stay." Then hopefully, "We stay?"

"The devil you'll stay! You're coming outside—now."

The Martians jabbered in a desert dialect, gesturing outside every now and then and shaking their heads nervously. But they shuffled forward in single file and headed for the airlock.

Suuki, who'd sought the black asteroid with an eagerness to match Perez', needed no prompting. He said, "Where do you keep the spacesuits?"

"We don't have any," Perez chuckled.

"Don't have any? How are we going outside?"

"WHY DON'T you just leave that to me? I told you I was here before. That black globe outside has gravity close to Earth-norm, and it has a good, breathable atmosphere."

Suuki scowled. "You wouldn't want to march us out there to suffocate us, would you?"

"Don't be ridiculous! I'm going with you. I told you the place has air."

"That's impossible."

"Yes? So are the Marties, and you Venusians for that matter."

"What do you mean?"

"Well, consider. On Earth, the dominant life form is human. What would you say were the odds against that happening on Mars as well, and on Venus?"

Suuki scratched his head. "I never thought of it that way. Now that you mention it, it does sound almost an impossibility."

"All I'm trying to say," Perez continued, "is that the impossible can happen. And perhaps if we knew all the facts, it wouldn't be impossible at all. There are slight physical differences, but men of the three worlds are essentially the same. Could it be that long ago the seeds were planted on each world, which would, in the natural course of events, evolve into something human? Could it also be that whoever—or whatever—planted those seeds also put this Asteroid here? Outside you'll see pictures of Earthmen, of Marties, of Venusians. But the asteroid is older than any of our races. That means they knew humanity was coming. If you set a tree shrew down on Earth sixty million years ago, you'd know that in the natural course of events its progeny would become human. Over a long path and with a lot of false starts, but once the pattern was set, mankind became inevitable. The same holds for Mars and Venus.

"Don't ask me how, don't ask me why. But whoever did that planting also planted this asteroid."

"It does look artificial," Ellen agreed.

"Of course it is! I figure they made it just before their planet exploded. You know these asteroids all once were part of a planet out here, perhaps one the size of Mercury or Pluto. But this thing is different. They left it here and I say that they knew it would one day be found. It has...and it's mine."

You couldn't argue with Perez logic, nor with the blaster he held in his hand.

UNTIL we actually stepped outside, I think Suuki still doubted. But the air was warm and good, although it had a musty smell. And Suuki—who'd doubted until he saw for himself—came up with the answer. Suuki was like that. "Naturally," he mused. "How could we have missed it? If the atoms of the upper atmosphere were somehow stripped of both protons and electrons, what you'd have left would be the inter-atomic forces which bind them together, or—"

"A perfect force-field for holding in the atmosphere!" Ellen finished for him.

It didn't mean much to the Martians. They clung close to the light fanning out from the nose of the ship, but this soon became a feeble glow lost behind us and the Martians cowered back toward it.

Perez bellowed: "Come on up here! Come on now! Snap to it."

They came, mumbling apologies. I looked at Suuki. Suuki looked at me. "I don't get it," I said. "They're scared stiff, but they obey Perez like he's a god."

Ellen laughed. "You don't know Martian custom. Look at it this way, the planet is one big rat race. There isn't enough water, there's even less food. Most Marties are scrawny bags of skin and bones. If one tribal chieftain becomes really powerful, he can eat well. He takes advantage of it. He gets fat, and because that clearly speaks of power, he becomes more powerful."

Suuki held his sides, roared with laughter. "That's rich!" he cried. "That's rich, but I see what you mean. Perez is the fattest man the Marties ever saw. Obviously then, to them he's a mighty ruler, and thus they obey him."

"Shut up," Perez growled back over his shoulder. "I heard that. If you think it's so funny, maybe I'll have the Marties flay you alive. They'll do it, too, if I ask them, you know."

"Nice guy," Ellen said.

I shook my head. "Cut it out. Perez isn't joking."

That brought us back to the situation in a hurry. Perez could kill us—and would if we caused him any trouble. On the other hand, he needed us. He knew that and when the time came it might stay his hand, but megalomania carries with it feelings both of power and persecution, and Perez could be a mighty deadly captor.

NOTHING gave underfoot as we walked. Nothing crunched. Instead, our boots click-clacked over a polished black surface, hard as marble. Perez snapped on a hand search beam and swaggered forward confidently. We came behind him, Suuki, Ellen and I—and in our rear were the Martians.

"We might jump him," Suuki hissed, bringing his head close to mine.

"We might, and it might not work. But that isn't the point. Perez looks like he knows where he's going. Okay, we'll follow."

Ahead of us, Perez had stopped. He probed about with the light for a time, grunted something unintelligible under his breath. He fastened the light to his belt, got down on hands and knees. In the glare of the search beam, an uneven splotch of paint gleamed dully.

Perez turned briefly and looked in my direction. "You don't remember, do you?"

"N—no."

"You made this, Boky, when you were here a couple of years ago. It marks u-uhh!"

Perez broke off in mid-sentence. His fat, clumsy fingers began to do a jig on the smooth black surface. Something clicked, faintly audible in the complete silence. Perez stood up and dusted off his hands.

The three Marties looked like they half-expected a fire-breathing dragon to push its way up from the rock. Ellen glanced at me for some signs of returning memory, but I shrugged and she turned her attention back to the surface of the asteroid. Suuki whistled.

A ten-foot section of polished black stone slid away!

CHAPTER SEVEN
Secret of the Black Globe

A SOFT amber radiance pulsed up through the aperture, apparently set off by whatever opened the trapdoor. A flight of stairs led down.

Perez called to the Martians. "All right. You first."

"No, masser. We stay."

Perez snorted angrily, then shrugged. This time, even his impressive bulk couldn't sway the Marties. I think he could have threatened them with death and their refusal to venture below would have remained unshaken.

He said: "You, first, Boky. Then the girl, then Suuki. I'll follow."

Slowly, I went down the stairs. Seven, eight, nine—I counted them. Nine steps. I heard Ellen start down behind me, but for a moment I forgot all about her, forgot Suuki and Perez and everything else.

Across a short hallway a mural had been painted on the wall. Half a dozen people, naked. An Earthman and his mate. Two Marties, male and female. Two Venusians. Completely realistic, all of them. They stood near what was evidently a spaceship of some alien design.

Suuki had reached bottom. "This must have been done recently," he said. "How else can you explain—"

"Don't be ridiculous!" This was Perez. "Don't you understand? See? See, they are pictured without clothing. Sixty million years ago the seed was planted, it was known humanity would develop on each of the three planets. It certainly could not be known what sort of clothing they would affect."

Ellen nodded. "This is ancient, Suuki—impossibly ancient. Johnny told me that in one of his messages, before he vanished."

Impatiently, Perez motioned us ahead of him down the hallway. We passed the mural, walked further, came to a wide archway. Beyond it was a great vault of a room. Tier upon tier of machinery lined the walls, climbed to the high ceiling.

Everything waiting, in repose—for sixty million years?

The strange machinery did not clutter up the place. It stood back against the four walls, polished, shining. In the center of the room rested a cup of metal, as wide across as the height of a tall man, and to this Perez ran eagerly.

"Do you remember, Boky? Think man, you must remember something!"

I DID. In a haze, like a dimly recalled dream, I remembered. "Yes," I mumbled, almost a part of that forgotten dream. "I stood here and I looked. I studied it, thought I understood. I remained down here—a long time. Somehow, I—I think my ship got loose from its moorings, floated off into space. Someone found me—"

"That's not what I mean!" Perez cried. "Do you remember anything about this place?"

"That—that's part of it, too. I remember the cup, the thing there in the center of the room. I sat in it. Yes, I sat there. I think you'll find a lever on the left side. I pulled it. I—that's it! I sat in the cup and I pulled the lever and then things started to happen…"

"It gave you this power of regeneration," Perez shouted triumphantly. He waddled toward the cup, peered at it for a moment, circled it, came back.

"I'm going to try it," he said at last.

I had a headache. Something was nagging at my brain, saying *remember, remember!* But it was there and then it was not, like the tides ebbing and flowing. "Don't," I said.

"Eh? Why not? I know—you're afraid someone else will get the power too…"

"N—no. I don't think so. I just know that you shouldn't, not before we understand this machine as I understood it once."

"Bah! You're lying." Perez lumbered back to the cup of metal, placed both hands on its rim and clambered up. He was panting when he finished, but he squatted within the cup.

"You're right, Boky. A lever on the left side. How I've waited for this…"

He made a motion with his left hand, kept the blaster pointed at us with his right.

A richer amber glow filled the inside of the cup as the banks of machinery along the four walls whined and grumbled into action. Wheels grated against wheels. Sparks flashed. Perez's laughter boomed through the vault as the amber glow bathed him, caressed him.

ABRUPTLY, it was over. The wheels stopped their turning, the glow faded. Perez came down from the cup and stalked ponderously across the room. "I feel wonderful," he said, still laughing half-hysterically. "I never felt better in my life. You don't believe me, eh? Then watch…"

With trembling fingers, Perez took a knife from his pocket, opened it, ran the blade across his wrist.

"He's insane!" Suuki cried.

"No." I shook my head. "Look now."

The blood began to flow, slowing to a trickle almost at once. When it stopped altogether, Perez wiped it off his fat arm with a handkerchief. Only the vaguest shadow of a scar remained. He held his arm up high so we could see it, waving his hand overhead almost like a victorious fighter. "See?" he demanded. "See—I'm a superman. You're a superman too, Boky—only you don't realize. There is so little that can destroy you, so little to keep you from owning the Three Worlds with the power that resides within this room."

"Yes?" demanded Suuki. "Then tell me how."

"Fool! I'll sell to the highest bidder. 'You too can become invulnerable,' I'll tell them. Provided they can pay. Oh, I'll make them pay. They'll beg the money, they'll steal it, they'll kill for it. But they'll pay."

It wasn't a pretty picture. Chaos would sweep the solar system, and I think Perez knew it. Here was a veritable immortality—if even only for a lifetime. Armies would fight for it. Brother would kill brother. And if Perez could somehow maintain control, he'd get his wish. He'd be lord and master of the entire Solar System.

IT WAS then that I knew he had to be destroyed. The thought did not come melodramatically. I felt nothing of the hero in me, nor of the noble urge to kill that others might live. The thought was just there, completely objective, and Perez had to die. Suuki nodded his head slowly, as if in some mysterious way the thought had passed between us.

But Perez had other ideas. "You will observe," he said slowly, "that I no longer have need for you. I thought you might in some way help me, but I was mistaken. It remains only to destroy you." He still held the blaster in his hands, toying with it, but he spoke as if to himself. "The girl I can kill and Suuki, too, but what can I do with you, Boky? Eh, that is a good question! I can't be sure, but I think that if I sear you completely from head to foot... Yes!"

He was the megalomaniac completely now, talking to himself, strutting about on his thick legs. "I believe I will let you decide. Which one is to die first?"

Ellen took my hand in hers, squeezed it. "Johnny, he isn't fooling. Johnny! I'm afraid—"

Suuki said, "I am not one to wait around. I grow bored. If you like, you may kill me first." He walked off half a dozen paces, folded his arms across his chest, and waited.

Perez chuckled, pivoted to face him, the blaster raised. For a moment, that took his eyes off me.

The slightest motion would attract his attention—and also death. He stood three yards away, sighting at Suuki's stomach, saying something about making it painless. I could do only one thing.

I left the floor completely and dove at him.

He whirled at the last instant, firing his blaster. Its beam seared air inches from my head and brought brief, burning pain with it. Then my shoulder jarred against his huge belly and we both tumbled to the floor.

I'M STRONG—but I got the shock of my life. You hear so much about people fighting like madmen, and you don't believe half of it. A cliché, that's all, with no more truth than—

But Perez *did* fight like a madman. His fists were everywhere, pounding, pummeling, gouging.

He used his feet, kicking with them and bringing his knee up at my groin. He butted with his head, jarring my teeth. He bit and clawed and scratched.

Dimly, I heard Ellen screaming. The blaster had clattered off somewhere across the floor, but she couldn't find it. And shock had set in for Suuki. He had been near death and he knew it, and for the moment he couldn't stir a muscle.

My knuckles were bruised and bleeding. I struck his face, hard stinging blows, anyone of which should have been enough to end it. I sat on his chest and beat at his head with both hands, but he turned and threw me off, jumped on me, held me down with his tremendous bulk. His hands sought my neck, found it and closed. His face swam in the amber light, back and forth, back and forth.

I reached out wildly, got the fleshy part of his jowls between my fingers. I tugged until I thought his face would come off in one piece. But I grew weaker every moment, a hollow, burning sensation flooding up from my starved lungs.

Perez laughed, howled, then laughed again. He screamed horribly and rolled over and away. I had time only for one deep breath, felt the wonderful cool air soothe my aching chest. Then I was on him again, hammering blows at his face and stomach while he kicked and bit and clawed and writhed. I hit him until my hands lost all sensation, I hit him with the two numb, swollen things attached to my wrists. He finally sighed, shut his eyes, and lay back unconscious.

Long ago I'd bathed in the metal cup. Perez had followed me into it this day. In five minutes we both felt fine, and, and we looked it, too. Except for the blood.

WE SAT in the control room of Perez's ship. It hadn't been hard to round up the Marties with Perez's blaster. We'd trussed them up neatly and tucked them into a storeroom.

Suuki said, "I still think we ought to kill him. He can't be permitted to live, not with the power he's got, and the ideas."

I nodded, but Ellen shook her head for the hundredth time. "No. You can't do it—that's all. This is the twenty-first century and men don't go around killing one another. There are laws for that."

"He can't live," Suuki persisted. "Please."

Suuki had been too stunned to act back in the vault. My hands had remained swollen for a few minutes. Thus, it had been Ellen who took the blaster from the floor and rounded up the Marties. Now she held it and she said: "Everything both of you say is true. Except for one thing: he goes back and he gets a trial. I think it can be proved that he killed Dr. Elkins, anyway."

Suuki shrugged and relented. "Well, I suppose we can't argue with you. We might as well—"

Perez chuckled. "You won't be able to prove a thing about Elkins. I...uh...had the Marties who disposed of him destroyed immediately after that. And since Marties are always killing one another with their vendettas—well, you figure it out."

Sanity had returned to Perez. He spoke rationally, objectively, without passion. Unfortunately, he knew what he was talking about.

Ellen told him to sit still and behave himself, prodding the flesh of his arm with her blaster. I guess Perez wanted to keep in her good graces. He shut up.

"Now, Johnny," Ellen turned to face me, "do you think you can piece everything together? What was that place?"

"An asteroid," I said. "But an artificial one. Near as I can figure it, this is what happened. Millions of years ago, this Solar System of ours was visited—from outside. They came, whoever they were, and they lived on the fifth planet, which now is a mess of cosmic debris. Okay so far?"

"Okay."

"They got busy fast. They planted on Earth, Mars, and Venus certain strains of animal life that would insure, in each case, the ultimate arrival of humanity by old Darwin's process of natural selection. Their evolutionary science was a great one, they could even tell what the future humans would be like—and they drew pictures to prove it. Maybe their job was to travel around the galaxy planting the human seed.

"Anyway, some time after that, something happened. War or some form of cosmic disaster. Their planet was destroyed, exploding completely, becoming the zone of asteroids that we know today. They left a record, that artificial globe. Don't you think it's significant that their picture showed the humans entering a spaceship? Somewhere in there is the secret not of interplanetary flight—but of interstellar flight. When we were ready, they figured, we could come out to the stars and visit them.

"OKAY SO FAR? Good. One of the secrets they left in that globe had to do with regeneration, with tissue that grew young again. Maybe it's tied in someplace with star travel, I don't know. But the last time I made a mistake. I should have informed the government right away, and I didn't. This time we'll let the brains of the solar system figure it out.

"Finally, there was a card put in my pocket last time. That puzzled me at first, but I think I can figure it out. One of those machines in there could read my mind, decipher the language it used, give me a written message in it. Sure, people would try to kill me. I'd have to be careful because I'd uncovered a mighty potent secret. The builders of that asteroid had wisdom beyond ours, and they knew it. They…"

I must have liked the sound of my own voice. I kept on talking and talking. But suddenly Ellen screamed.

She was staring at Perez, and I looked too. I don't know how old Perez was—thirty-five, maybe forty. Sitting on the floor of the control room, he looked sixteen!

Still fat, but baby-faced. Now he said, "I don't understand. What's happening? Good lord, what's happening to me?"

His voice was in the changing stage, squeaking on every third or fourth word.

Shuttered, the port windows make good mirrors. Perez staggered to one and we didn't stop him. He looked—saw the reflection of a fat boy of sixteen.

No—fourteen. Twelve.

As we watched, he grew smaller. Smaller.

A child of seven, still extremely fat!

"Please!" he moaned in a high childish treble. "What's happening?"

He became too small for his clothing, stepped out of it. He was crying, big tears rolling down his pink cheeks.

"By the gods of Karn," muttered Suuki. "What on—"

"I remember!" I cried. "I remember!" No one paid me any heed. They were busy watching the small boy Perez grow smaller. And younger. "See?" I said. "I remember. I studied the machine that first time. A small dose meant regeneration. A larger dose meant *rejuvenation*. Same process, tissues rebuilding themselves instantly. Perez took too much. It will go on and on…"

A tiny infant, naked and very pink of skin, lay crying on the floor. Its face looked intelligent, but it was a very fat infant. It looked like it wanted to say something, but all it could do was scream.

The ugly pink face grew smaller, the eyes clamped shut.

The infant rolled over on its side, legs and arms curling up, assuming the fetal position. Then the body grew smaller, but the head didn't. Something long and thin protruded from the abdomen, like a slender pink strip of rope.

Sobbing, Ellen threw herself into my arms, buried her face against my chest. "Oh Johnny, Johnny! How awful!"

I stroked her hair, took her to a chair and sat her down gently. When I returned, Suuki's face was very white. The infant had vanished.

"It got smaller," Suuki mumbled to himself. "And smaller. It didn't look human any longer. It shrunk to a tiny glob finally, amorphous, then small and round I think. It got smaller. It disappeared, I think—I think I shall be sick, John. I hope you do not mind. Perez was more than rejuvenated. Perez kept right on going. He became an infant. A fetus. Less than a fetus. He became—nothing…"

WE LANDED at New York Spaceport, and I've never seen anything that looked quite as wonderful as the rolling hills of Westchester.

"The Government will send men out there," I told Ellen as I helped her down. "They can find a lot that's good or a lot that's evil on that asteroid. It depends upon their own point of view. But one thing I know."

"What's that?"

"Somehow, someway—there's the power to reach the stars on that little black globe. A whole new universe waits for man out there. And it won't be waiting long. Just a generation or so."

"You mean our children?"

"Uh-huh."

"Well, I hope you mean that literally. I mean, well—" She began to blush.

But Suuki was laughing. "By the gods of Karn, you'd better marry that girl! She won't give you a moment's rest until you do."

And so we've been married half a year already. Ellen's busy planning and knitting, but every day she stops to ask me if I know what Johnny, Jr. will be like. And we dream of what he'll possibly discover on the Black Planet.

THE END

If you've enjoyed this book, you will not want to miss these terrific titles...

ARMCHAIR SCI-FI & HORROR DOUBLE NOVELS, $12.95 each

D-11 **PERIL OF THE STARMEN** by Kris Neville
THE STRANGE INVASION by Murray Leinster

D-12 **THE STAR LORD** by Boyd Ellanby
CAPTIVES OF THE FLAME by Samuel R. Delany

D-13 **MEN OF THE MORNING STAR** by Edmond Hamilton
PLANET FOR PLUNDER by Hal Clement and Sam Merwin, Jr.

D-14 **ICE CITY OF THE GORGON** by Chester S. Geier and Richard Shaver
WHEN THE WORLD TOTTERED by Lester Del Rey

D-15 **WORLDS WITHOUT END** by Clifford D. Simak
THE LAVENDER VINE OF DEATH by Don Wilcox

D-16 **SHADOW ON THE MOON** by Joe Gibson
ARMAGEDDON EARTH by Geoff St. Reynard

D-17 **THE GIRL WHO LOVED DEATH** by Paul W. Fairman
SLAVE PLANET by Laurence M. Janifer

D-18 **SECOND CHANCE** by J. F. Bone
MISSION TO A DISTANT STAR by Frank Belknap Long

D-19 **THE SYNDIC** by C. M. Kornbluth
FLIGHT TO FOREVER by Poul Anderson

D-20 **SOMEWHERE I'LL FIND YOU** by Milton Lesser
THE TIME ARMADA by Fox B. Holden

ARMCHAIR SCIENCE FICTION CLASSICS, $12.95 each

C-4 **CORPUS EARTHLING**
by Louis Charbonneau

C-5 **THE TIME DISSOLVER**
by Jerry Sohl

C-6 **WEST OF THE SUN**
by Edgar Pangborn

ARMCHAIR SCIENCE FICTION & HORROR GEMS SERIES, $12.95 each

G-1 **SCIENCE FICTION GEMS, Vol. One**
Isaac Asimov and others

G-2 **HORROR GEMS, Vol. One**
Carl Jacobi and others

If you've enjoyed this book, you will not want to miss these terrific titles...

ARMCHAIR SCI-FI, FANTASY, & HORROR DOUBLE NOVELS, $12.95 each

D-21　**EMPIRE OF EVIL** by Robert Arnette
　　　　THE SIGN OF THE TIGER by Alan E. Nourse & J. A. Meyer

D-22　**OPERATION SQUARE PEG** by Frank Belknap Long
　　　　ENCHANTRESS OF VENUS by Leigh Brackett

D-23　**THE LIFE WATCH** by Lester Del Rey
　　　　CREATURES OF THE ABYSS by Murray Leinster

D-24　**LEGION OF LAZARUS** by Edmond Hamilton
　　　　STAR HUNTER by Andre Norton

D-25　**EMPIRE OF WOMEN** by John Fletcher
　　　　ONE OF OUR CITIES IS MISSING by Irving Cox

D-26　**THE WRONG SIDE OF PARADISE** by Raymond F. Jones
　　　　THE INVOLUNTARY IMMORTALS by Rog Phillips

D-27　**EARTH QUARTER** by Damon Knight
　　　　ENVOY TO NEW WORLDS by Keith Laumer

D-28　**SLAVES TO THE METAL HORDE** by Milton Lesser
　　　　HUNTERS OUT OF TIME by Joseph E. Kelleam

D-29　**RX JUPITER SAVE US** by Ward Moore
　　　　BEWARE THE USURPERS by Geoff St. Reynard

D-30　**SECRET OF THE SERPENT** by Don Wilcox
　　　　CRUSADE ACROSS THE VOID by Dwight V. Swain

ARMCHAIR SCIENCE FICTION CLASSICS, $12.95 each

C-7　**THE SHAVER MYSTERY, Book One**
　　　by Richard S. Shaver

C-8　**THE SHAVER MYSTERY, Book Two**
　　　by Richard S. Shaver

C-9　**MURDER IN SPACE** by David V. Reed
　　　by David V. Reed

ARMCHAIR MASTERS OF SCIENCE FICTION SERIES, $16.95 each

M-3　**MASTERS OF SCIENCE FICTION, Vol. Three**
　　　Robert Sheckley, "The Perfect Woman" and other tales

M-4　**MASTERS OF SCIENCE FICTION, Vol. Four**
　　　Mack Reynolds, "Stowaway" and other tales

If you've enjoyed this book, you will not want to miss these terrific titles...

If you've enjoyed this book, you will not want to miss these terrific titles…

ARMCHAIR SCI-FI & HORROR DOUBLE NOVELS, $12.95 each

D-51 **A GOD NAMED SMITH** by Henry Slesar
WORLDS OF THE IMPERIUM by Keith Laumer

D-52 **CRAIG'S BOOK** by Don Wilcox
EDGE OF THE KNIFE by H. Beam Piper

D-53 **THE SHINING CITY** by Rena M. Vale
THE RED PLANET by Russ Winterbotham

D-54 **THE MAN WHO LIVED TWICE** by Rog Phillips
VALLEY OF THE CROEN by Lee Tarbell

D-55 **OPERATION DISASTER** by Milton Lesser
LAND OF THE DAMNED by Berkeley Livingston

D-56 **CAPTIVE OF THE CENTAURIANESS** by Poul Anderson
A PRINCESS OF MARS by Edgar Rice Burroughs

D-57 **THE NON-STATISTICAL MAN** by Raymond F. Jones
MISSION FROM MARS by Rick Conroy

D-58 **INTRUDERS FROM THE STARS** by Ross Rocklynne
FLIGHT OF THE STARLING by Chester S. Geier

D-59 **COSMIC SABOTEUR** by Frank M. Robinson
LOOK TO THE STARS by Willard Hawkins

D-60 **THE MOON IS HELL!** by John W. Campbell, Jr.
THE GREEN WORLD by Hal Clement

ARMCHAIR SCIENCE FICTION CLASSICS, $12.95 each

C-16 **THE SHAVER MYSTERY, Book Three**
by Richard S. Shaver

C-17 **THE PLANET STRAPPERS**
by Raymond Z. Gallun

C-18 **THE FOURTH "R"**
by George O. Smith

ARMCHAIR SCIENCE FICTION & HORROR GEMS SERIES, $12.95 each

G-5 **SCIENCE FICTION GEMS, Vol. Three**
C. M. Kornbluth and others

G-6 **HORROR GEMS, Vol. Three**
August Derleth and others

THE SECRETS OF SPACE-TIME TRAVEL!

The Corporations of Terra were locked in a deadly battle to wrest control from the Government. The mysteries of space-time travel had finally been discovered and were now ready to be tested. But the many spies for General Atomic were closing in fast on the Government's men, but Jon Saxon was not your average government man. He had certain powers that were far beyond those of the average man. Extra-sensory powers.

Accompany Jon Saxon and his eccentric crew of specialists, onlookers, and mutineers as they hurtle across the deep void of space toward Alpha Centauri— toward yet another world of intrigue and manipulation in this fantastic tale of interstellar flight and the darkest secrets of mankind's origins.

CAST OF CHARACTERS

JON SAXON
This government scientist and agent was a man of extraordinary character—and extraordinary senses.

ILETH URBAN
She was sexy, alluring, the perfect bait—and it was well known that Q62 controlled her every action, but no one knew why…

DR. JOHN VILLAINOWSKI
He had discovered the secret of space-time travel…along with the experience known as "The Little Death."

GAVIN MURDOCK
This government liaison for the expedition to Alpha Centauri was finding his fellow passengers and crew somewhat…suspicious.

MERCEDES
She was the expedition's lone anthropologist—and as it turned out, one of the lone dissenters to mutiny.

CLO-JAVEL
Being a noted archaeologist, she knew damn well that a perfect replica of NYC could not be found on another planet!

THE MODERATOR
He was an alien elder deeply concerned about his "experiment," which he determined needed to come to an end—now!

THE
OUTCASTS OF
SOLAR III

By
EMMETT McDOWELL

ARMCHAIR FICTION
PO Box 4369, Medford, Oregon 97501-0168

CHAPTER ONE

"QUIET," JON SAXON'S VOICE was a breath in the night as he cautioned the girl. A warning prickle of danger had run over his skin like gooseflesh. He was a big man, over six feet, with thick brawny shoulders and arms like a blacksmith. Before the girl could cry out, Saxon swept her into the deep shadow of a doorway. His dark gray eyes probed the street but he could see no one.

This seventh level thoroughfare of Adirondaka appeared utterly deserted. Only occasional street lamps revealed glimpses of the magnificent architecture of the post-atom capitol of Earth. Down the center of the boulevard the public conveyor swept silently, endlessly without a passenger anywhere along its ribbon-like length.

"Where are they?" the girl whispered.

He shook his head. "I can't see them." But his skin continued to prickle its warning. Somewhere in the shadows were men, several of them, stalking him soundlessly.

He became aware of an alien quality about the figures ringing in him and the girl, figures he could sense but not see. Still nothing moved in the street. The girl, he realized, was strangely quiescent.

Then, sharp as speech, her thought impinged on Jon Saxon's consciousness. *The fools! And after I told Emil not to let them crowd him!*

Jon Saxon's eyes narrowed. So the girl thought the invisible figures were G. A.'s men. He had known, of course, from their first meeting that the girl was a General Atomic spy. But by not so much as a hint had he let her suspect that her very thoughts betrayed her.

The tingling sensation intensified, warned him that the shadows were closing in. The feel of alienism was stronger, as if they were not quite human. His heart pumped faster, the pulse throbbing in his ears.

The moon was rising, he saw, competing indifferently with the streetlights. Its rays streamed down through the ninety-eight levels of the capitol, down through crystal plastic roadways into the dense blackness of the pit itself.

Again he became aware of the girl's thought, *"Why, there's nothing here! He's imagining things!"* It was accompanied by a wave of relief, and at the same time she whispered.

"What is it Jon? What do you see?"

"Hold it, Ileth!"

His hands gripped her slender shoulders, silenced her. The public conveyor still swept past without a sound.

Bewilderment grew in him.

The alien entities were close, all about them, apparently without substance. The tingling sensations were like hot and cold flashes now, signaling him of something present, something that he couldn't identify.

They were not the girl's men, whatever she thought. He would have recognized them by their feel.

No, these escaped classification. He had never experienced anything like them before. His strange sixth sense, the first extra-human sense that he had begun to develop inexplicably in his twenty-seventh year, could perceive nothing beyond their presence.

He took his hand from Ileth's shoulders, groped for the button controlling the door against which they crouched.

"Stop!"

The thought rang like a bell in his skull.

Jon Saxon stiffened. *"What is it?"* he concentrated. *"Who are you?"*

Again the bodiless thought struck into his mind.

"That is not for you to know—now or possibly ever. The girl is working for General Atomic. Do not allow yourself to be duped. It is decidedly not our policy that General Atomic or any of the corporations learn the secret of the stellar drive!"

SAXON'S eyes opened with surprise. He had no intention of giving G. A. the secret of the stellar drive. It was a government secret, for one thing...

"We are quite aware of your intentions," came the telepathic communication. *"Otherwise, you would no longer be."*

Saxon swallowed dryly, realized his palms were sweating. He glanced at Ileth. The moonlight had crept into the doorway, illuminating her oval face clearly. He noted the perplexed slant to her fine dark brows, the sober, half-frightened expression clouding her patrician features.

"Why don't we go?" she asked. "What are you waiting for?"

"In a minute."

He sent his thought probing out toward the alien minds. And was brought up sharp before an absolute mental barrier.

No neophytes here. Whatever the creatures were, they were masters of thought transference. Excitement sent the blood surging through Saxon's veins, blotted out momentarily his alarm.

Until this moment, he had believed himself unique, the single telepath on Earth.

He had been thirty-one when he first became aware of his telepathic potential. It had developed overnight, a seventh extra-human sense that isolated him forever from the rest of mankind.

There had been something indecent, prying about seeing into the minds of his fellows—like a peeping Tom. It had been intolerable at first, the naked baring of souls before him, intolerable and shocking, until he had learned to block out their thoughts.

He felt the girl shiver against him.

"But what are you afraid of, Jon?"

He didn't answer because the alien thoughts intruded on his mind again.

"This is a warning, Jon Saxon. Do not divulge the stellar drive to anyone. It is not and never was intended for you to know. Only the unfortunate development of a telepathic sense enabled you to steal it from Villainowski's brain…"

"I didn't steal it!" Saxon thought indignantly. *"I worked with Villainowski building the ship. It would have been impossible for me not to learn it."*

"Exactly," came the reply. *"And your continued existence hinges entirely on your silence."*

A chill wind blew up Saxon's spine, but it only fanned the flame of eagerness, which had sprung up in within him. Here were others like himself, possessed of telepathic powers.

"Who are you?" he thought passionately.

He realized in dismay that the prickling in skin and scalp had diminished. The telepaths were withdrawing, deserting him without a hint of further contact.

"Who are you? How can I find you?"

Nothing!

He and the girl were alone again in the moonlit doorway.

A strange sense of exhilaration replaced Saxon's first feeling of letdown. There were other telepaths on Earth and sometime, someplace their paths would cross again. He stepped into the street, saying to Ileth, "Let's go. I was mistaken. There's no one here."

In the rays of the street lamp, he looked more like a pugilist than a Government Bureau of Research man and one of Terra's top nuclear physicists. He had a big nose, twice broken, strong white teeth and a square massive jaw. He caught the girl's thought and grinned down at her.

"*He's not handsome,*" she was thinking, "*not by any standard, but when he grins like that you don't think about his looks and virility radiates from him like heat waves. He's a dangerous man! Emil underrates him!*"

"Hadn't we better take the conveyor?" she asked aloud.

JON SAXON nodded, swung the girl lightly by her elbows to the pick-up, transferred to commuter, then express. They found seats while the buildings flowed past on either hand like a speeded-up movie.

"You have a frightening job," said Ileth, looking up at his from big hazel-green eyes. Her shiny dark red hair she wore in a shoulder length pageboy bob. She smoothed her short-waisted chartreuse jacket over small firm breasts. "I'm surprised Government lets you go out without your bodyguard."

"They don't." Saxon's unprepossessing features lit with a boyish grin. "But I slip away from them once in a while."

"You were afraid of an ambush back there in the street?"

He nodded. "Yes. I thought one of the corporations may have got wind of my escapade."

The girl, he saw from her thoughts, was satisfied with his explanation.

In these days of savage competition, the big corporations maintained their own factories and laboratories. General Atomic, Tri-World, Amalgamated Plastic, a score of lesser companies employed staffs of technicians and research scientists. The lives of these men were fraught with a peculiar danger. They were subject to bribery, kidnapping and torture by the spy agencies of rival companies in their efforts to extort from them any new discovery or guarded scientific process their corporations might possess. Independent agencies manned by corrupt technicians had men everywhere.

The corporations protected themselves by confining their technicians to barracks and never permitting them to wander forth unescorted. It was a condition, which Jon Saxon found little better than slavery. The constant surveillance irked him to the point of rebellion.

Now he was confronted suddenly with the fact that he had been under observation of an infinitely more subtle kind as well. Some group was keeping constant watch upon his mind. But who?

Ileth sighed and laid her head on his shoulder. "Jon, you've been so quiet tonight. Is it because tomorrow the expedition leaves for Alpha Centauri?"

"I don't know. I'm not afraid, exactly. We know the drive is practicable, but it's the first attempt man's ever made to reach the stars. We've never been beyond the Solar System before, Ileth."

He felt the girl's arms slip around his neck, cling with surprising strength. "I'm afraid, Jon. I wish you weren't going."

"What are you afraid of?"

Ileth bit her lower, lip. She was feeling rather than thinking, Saxon realized, a mental chaos bubbling in the primitive thalamic regions of her nervous system, a formless intuition of disaster stalking the first expedition into stellar space.

"I—I don't know exactly," she confessed. "I don't understand it, Jon."

Saxon's eyes narrowed. He had intercepted that dread of the expedition's fate before. He had felt it emanating from hundreds of individuals otherwise unrelated. It was like a hypnotically imposed command: *"Don't venture into the Stellar Depths!"*

And it always stemmed from the subconscious, the regions of the human mind telepathically closed to him. At first he'd been inclined to think it was dread of the unknown. But now he was not so sure.

Facts, Saxon knew, were assimilated by the subconscious, later to emerge as hunches and intuition. He had grown to believe that there must be reason behind this universal fear of stellar space.

He had even felt it in himself; in his chief, Villainowski; in his co-workers at Government's Bureau of Research. It was a very real feeling that nothing but disaster for the human race could come of this venture to the stars.

CHAPTER TWO

ILETH'S APARTMENT WAS ON the ninety-eighth level, flush against the transparent plastic dome, which hermetically sealed in Adirondaka.

Jon Saxon followed the girl out of the lift, watching her with admiration.

She was a slim, long legged creature in chartreuse green, jodhpur-like trousers that molded her slender waist and rounded hips with amazing fidelity before flaring at her thighs.

Ileth Urban was as fetching a bit of scientist-bait, as General Atomic could have desired.

All the corporations used these girls. They scoured the Solar System for the cleverest, most beautiful ones to be found. They paid them fantastic wages and trained them to worm secrets from susceptible males. Scientific Mata Hari's.

Government itself used them, Saxon was fully aware. Only by employing even more ruthless measures than the corporations was government able to maintain itself. Government had the finest research department anywhere. And the Terrestrial Intelligence Service was the most efficient organization of its kind. Not only that; Government had power, power unbelievable in its Space Navy.

Ileth paused, allowing him to come abreast of her, her hazel-green eyes smiling at him.

Saxon hastily blocked out her thoughts in embarrassment. *"You're a pretty little Judas,"* he thought, then glanced up as a bright glare lit the night sky.

A trail of orange flame streaked above the city and disappeared like a meteor in reverse. The *Morning Star*, a crack luxury liner, was heading out for Venus. It must be nineteen hours.

"Our last night," said Ileth softly. "Tomorrow we'll be leaving for Alpha Centauri like that ship."

They had reached a door in the glistening plastic face of a building. The door opened automatically, responsive to the girl's personal vibration.

Saxon saw a lambent darkness beyond the entrance. The ceiling of Ileth's apartment was the transparent rind of the city itself. The moon streamed through the crystal plastic, lighting it faintly.

His nerves tightened, his sixth sense of feel exploring the apartment for a trap.

But no warning tingle prickled his skin. Then the lights came on as Ileth passed inside. They glowed from the walls like cold flame.

With a sigh of relief, Saxon saw that the chamber was empty.

"Sit down," said Ileth, "I'll get you a drink." She disappeared through a doorway across the room, stripping her yellow green jacket from her shoulders as she went.

Jon Saxon sank onto a lounge, following Ileth's progress by her thoughts.

"Soda. Where's that soda? Oh, here it is. Emil must have put it there. Like a man." Then, *"Contact Emil?"*

A moment's indecision. Saxon could almost hear the girl thinking. *"Not yet,"* she decided with a mental shiver. *"Saxon would be no good to us dead."* Then, *"Make the drink strong. Take a gallon to make him drunk. Big brute. Shoulders like a door. I could..."*

Saxon hastily blocked out her thought in embarrassment. The girl's mind was too graphic.

For the hundredth time his brain grappled with the identity of those alien telepaths who had warned him in the street tonight.

The radiation branch of Government's Bureau of Research had been experimenting with thought projection. Could they have been successful? It might account for the alien feel he had experienced for that impenetrable barrier which had defeated his attempt to reach their minds.

A machine?

Unconsciously, he shook his head. His sixth sense, the ability not only to feel a presence but identify it almost as if he were seeing it convinced him that there had been life in the street, a strange invisible form of life possibly; but the reality of it was inescapable. In some ways his heightened sense of feel was more reliable than his ears or eyes.

Ileth returned bearing a tray with glasses, a decanter of whiskey and soda. "I wasn't long, was I?"

THERE was a hard bright glitter in her hazel-green eyes. Saxon saw that she had changed to a halter and skirt of Martian microweb. He swallowed, feeling a pulse beginning to tick in his throat. The microweb was as red as the girl's hair, but not anywhere so thick.

Only her cold determination to keep him there until after the sailing, which he could feel like a dash of cold water, defeated her purpose.

She handed him a glass, set the tray on an end table, switched on the telecaster.

Instead of music, the newscaster was blaring forth the announcement of the expedition to Alpha Centauri.

"...greatest page in the annals of the Empire. Tomorrow at nine hours the *Shooting Star* with a picked crew, with a staff of specialists and representatives from all the great corporations will blast off for Alpha Centauri.

"Under the directorship of John Villainowski of Government's Bureau of Research, the man who developed the stellar drive, the expedition plans to investigate the planetary systems of the Centaurian suns.

"His Excellency, Mustapha IX, will be present..."

Ileth snapped off the telecaster.

"Jon," she asked and leaned against him, "why did you sneak out tonight of all nights?"

He sensed the girl's tension, knew that it would be difficult to fool her. Suddenly, he decided to quit beating around the bush and strike straight into the heart of the opposing forces.

"I know you're an agent of General Atomic, Ileth. I've..." He paused.

Ileth had gasped and drawn back from him. Her thoughts were in turmoil. *Emil! I must reach Emil!* was clear.

Saxon went on inexorably. "I've wind of a plot by General Atomic against the *Shooting Star.* If they could get their hands on the stellar drive, no doubt they could control deep space. They'd be in a position to dictate to Government."

Ileth was thinking furiously now, Saxon realized, trying to figure how much he knew and how much he was guessing.

He laughed without amusement. He knew damned little, too damned little.

Only this morning, he had intercepted the stray thought of one of his co-workers and realized that the man had sold out to General Atomic. To his horror he had read in the man's mind how General Atomic, after securing the stellar drive, intended to overthrow Government.

How General Atomic planned to get the drive, whom else was in the plot, the man hadn't known. He had been bribed to take orders from a GA agent, whom he knew only as Q62.

Saxon couldn't inform the T.I.S. of his knowledge. He had no proof, except what he had read in this one man's mind.

He had told Villainowski of his suspicions. The chief had promised to set the T.I.S. onto the case, but they had turned up no evidence of any kind against the great corporation.

General Atomic had done its work with utmost secrecy, not letting its right hand know what its left hand was doing.

Saxon was desperate. He grasped the girl's slight shoulders. "What do you know about it, Ileth?"

"I don't know anything. Oh Lord, Jon, I'm to be General Atomic's representative aboard the *Shooting Star,* and they've told me nothing of any plot against the ship. Nothing, Jon, I swear it."

With a disheartening feeling of defeat, Jon realized the girl was telling the truth. She had been told nothing of General Atomic's plan. She, too, he read in her frightened thoughts, had been instructed to take orders from a General Atomic's agent whom she knew as Q62.

"Who's Q62?" he shot at her.

Ileth's hazel-green eyes were enormous. "You! How did you know?"

"Who's Q62?"

"I don't know. I've never met him."

"How will you know him?"

"I don't know. They said he would be able to identify himself. That's all. They wouldn't tell me how."

All at once Saxon's skin began to prickle its warning of danger. He released the girl, wheeled towards the door just as it was flung viciously back.

He saw three men in the opening and reached for his dart gun.

With a half sob, Ileth hurled herself on him, bearing him backward to the couch, her arms around his chest, her long legs tangled with his.

"Emil!" she panted. "Quick! He's got a gun!"

"Easy. Easy. Easy," said a man's low amused voice.

Jon Saxon succeeded in throwing Ileth off his chest and surging to his feet. He found himself staring into the tiny barrel of a dart gun. The dart gun was being held steady as a rock by a gray-eyed, yellow-haired man with a faint smile on his wide thin lips.

Saxon let his hand fall away from his holster.

"Get his gun, Ileth."

"Right, Emil."

Saxon felt the girl's cool fingers slip inside his blouse, pluck his automatic from his holster.

"Has he any other weapons?"

She patted Saxon deftly, impersonally, shook her head, her dark red hair swinging.

"No. That's all."

The blond man lowered his gun. "You may sit down, sir."

Saxon sat down.

THERE were two others behind the blond man but Saxon kept his eyes on Emil, recognizing a dangerous type. Obviously well educated, intelligent, the blond man was fiercely loyal to General Atomic.

Not such a queer combination in these times, Saxon thought; when the corporations had come to replace countries in men's loyalties.

The anarchist revolt against Bureaucratic-Socialism had seriously weakened Terra and corporate business had fought its way back to power. Determined never again to permit the sacred laws of property to be so violated, it had fastened its tentacles to the very roots of society. It organized a government in an image of itself—a corporate government.

Men became known no longer as American or Spanish but as General Atomic men, or Tri-World men, or Corporate Government men and were as blindly patriotic to their corporations as they had been in earlier ages to the lands of their birth.

Such a one, Saxon recognized, was Emil of General Atomic, a fanatic who would consider it the greatest honor to die for his company.

"You realize, sir," said Emil, "that we regret very much what we must do."

"Why do it, then?" Jon Saxon asked bluntly.

The blond Emil looked shocked. "Are you suggesting treason, sir?"

"I'm not suggesting anything," replied Saxon, who had already read his death sentence in Emil's brain. "But you don't expect me to give you any information, when you plan to kill me immediately after."

Emil's expression was vaguely disturbed. "Nonsense! I'm commissioned to offer you a post in General Atomic's research department at twice your present salary, if you can give us the information we wish."

But Saxon still read nothing but inexorable death in Emil's mind.

"Eyewash," he said.

In the ensuing silence the men's thoughts beat at Saxon's brain like the confusing racket of people talking all at once.

At length Emil moved aside, saying, "We're prepared for obstinacy. Georg, take over."

A plump man of middle age drew up a chair facing Saxon.

"Georg," explained Emil, "is an N.P.A." Saxon stared into the moon-faced neural-psychoanalyst. The man possessed the most unusual pair of twinkling blue eyes like bits of glass, a smooth pink face, thin sandy hair. He was dressed like Emil in loose, comfortable coveralls of a gray siliconex.

He took Saxon's wrist, said pleasantly, "Hmmm, pulse rapid but strong. Unusual nervous control. Strip to the waist, if you please."

As Saxon pulled off his blouse, the plump N.P.A. turned to the third man, obviously his assistant, and said, "Bring the machine, Alph."

The man called Alph lugged a heavy case in front of the couch, opened it. Georg began to attach saucer shaped suction discs to Saxon's temples, the base of his skull, his solar plexus. Wires led from the discs to the machine in the black case.

"Quite ready," said Georg to Emil. "Ask any questions you wish."

Saxon could feel a delicate tingle rippling up his spine into his brain like a mild electric shock. Emil asked, "Do you know the secret of Villainowski's stellar drive?"

"No," returned Saxon. "That's preposterous. No one understands that except Villainowski himself. Do you think Government would be so stupid as to let the secret out?"

The plump N.P.A. who had been studying a bank of dials, looked up and said, "He's lying. From that I would infer that he understands the stellar drive."

"What?" gasped Emil.

With a sinking heart Jon Saxon realized that the blond man had not been expecting such luck. They had thought that he might be able to give them some clue to the stellar drive, but not that he actually could reproduce it.

"What's his torture coefficient?" Emil shot at the N.P.A.

Georg adjusted several dials. The tingling became livid fire coursing up Saxon's spine. His eyes closed, he crushed his lips between his teeth until a trickle of blood coursed down his chin.

The room swayed sickeningly. Sweat burst from his pores, made his sick white face glisten in the indirect lighting.

Then as sudden as it came, the fire smoldered and died out of his spine.

He heard the N.P.A. speak in an awed voice, "His torture coefficient is below his will to live. He'll die first."

EMIL began to stride nervously back and forth before the lounge. He swung suddenly on Saxon, saying, "Look, that post on General Atomic's research bureau is still open. I can promise you three times your present salary, and a bonus besides."

"Liar," replied Saxon without hesitation. "I don't need a machine to tell you're lying." He laughed shortly.

The N.P.A.'s plump face looked puzzled. He made rapid adjustments on the machine, bent over the dials again.

"He's not lying," he said in a queer voice. "He knows you intend to kill him as soon as you squeeze him dry of information."

Saxon caught sight of Ileth's white, strained face and grinned at her. She had been as surprised as himself at Emil's opportune entrance. Obviously, Emil had not been supposed to put in an appearance until she had a try at him first.

It was all verification that General Atomic was trying to steal the stellar drive. But Saxon had been able to catch only the scantiest of details from Emil's mind.

General Atomic not only wanted the drive, he sensed, but a monopoly on it. That meant killing or buying off everyone in Government's Bureau of Research who knew the secret of the drive.

Emil said to Saxon, "Suppose I contact General Atomic and put it up to them. I'll confess my orders were to question you, then dispose of you. Frankly, Ileth's reports have convinced us that you couldn't be bought."

"What makes you think that I can now? Anyway, what guarantee have I that their promises aren't as empty as yours?" he asked skeptically.

Georg, the neuro-psychoanalyst, pursed thick lips and interjected himself into the conversation. "General Atomic abides by its contracts," he pointed out.

"Yes. When it's to their advantage."

Emil's eyes blazed; red stained his pale cheek. "Do you mean to imply, sir, that General Atomic is treacherous?"

"Exactly."

"Emil!" said the plump N.P.A., sharply.

Slowly the flush receded from Emil's cheeks, but he held himself stiff as a ramrod and his eyes were angry.

The N.P.A. turned back to Saxon. "At least, you admit that General Atomic abides by its contracts as long as it's to their advantage."

Saxon nodded, seeing already what was coming.

"Then," pursued Georg. "It certainly would be to their advantage to preserve you alive until you could build a stellar drive. After that..." He shrugged. "You're an intelligent man, Saxon. Rated one of the best physicists in the Empire, in fact. It seems to me that you could easily convince General Atomic that it would be of advantage to them to keep you alive indefinitely. What would you say to a hundred thousand credits a year?"

"Not enough."

"Two hundred thousand?"

"One or two..." Saxon began, then paused in consternation. He had been tricked!

There was a self-satisfied smile on the neuro-psychoanalyst's pudgy features. He had not spoken aloud the words, "Two hundred thousand," but had thought them at Saxon!

"He's a telepath!" said the N.P.A., and began to disconnect the discs from Saxon's body and stow them back in the case.

"A telepath!" Emil ejaculated. "He's a telepath?"

"Exactly," agreed the N.P.A. in dry tones. "I suspected it from the first, but frankly I couldn't believe it. I've never encountered a true telepath before. I didn't think there were any. Individuals who are unusually canny at reading expression, yes. But never any true telepaths. I'm going to request General Atomic to let me perform an autopsy after he's been disposed of. Possibly he's a mutant."

"Disposed of?" ejaculated the blond Emil. "But great stars, Georg! He's invaluable to us. Not only does he possess the secret of the stellar drive, but he can…"

"You're the executive!" retorted Georg sharply, "but I advise you to shoot him now! This second!"

"What do you mean?"

"You're not stupid, man! How much information has he picked from our brains already? If he should escape, the plan would have to be sacrificed. Everything might be lost." Then, sharply, "And don't think about the plan! Shoot him!"

Saxon could read growing conviction in the blond man's mind. He saw Emil's hand, holding the dart gun, begin to rise.

"Look out, Emil!" shrieked Ileth suddenly.

But Saxon had already snatched the plump N.P.A. off his feet, yanking him between himself and Emil. He heard a sharp plop. The N.P.A.'s body quivered as it intercepted Emil's poisoned dart. Saxon realized he was holding aloft a dead man.

The muscles in his burly naked shoulders hunched. He hurled the dead N.P.A. at the blond man who went down, bowled over backwards by the body.

Emil's head struck the plastic floor with a sickening crunch. Saxon caught a painful mental flash as unconsciousness gripped the blond man.

Without a pause, he leaped for Ileth. The girl was fumbling at her waist, where her gun's muzzle had become entangled. Only the fact that the muzzle had caught in her waistband saved him.

She flinched back as Saxon's hand closed on the gun, tore it loose from her grip. There was a rip of cloth and the dart gun came away. Ileth's skirt, freed of its supporting waistband, slid down about her ankles.

Saxon leaped backward, threatening the N.P.A.'s flabbergasted assistant as well as the girl.

"Don't move! Either of you."

The N.P.A.'s assistant was obviously terrified and had no intention of budging.

"*Oh, my skirt!*" Ileth's wild thought came clear as a bell to Saxon, and the girl rolled her eyes toward her feet, where the cloth lay in a black ring. But she didn't move.

Saxon grinned. "Obviously," he said, "you haven't any weapon concealed about yourself. You can pick up your skirt, Ileth."

She snatched it about her waist again, holding the foot long tear together with her hand.

"I'm leaving," he said, "but remember, I can read your thoughts. If either of you make a move towards that audio during the next ten minutes, I'll pop back in and fill you as full of darts as a porcupine."

And he backed, still grinning, through the door.

CHAPTER THREE

THE HUGE STRUCTURE, housing Government's Bureau of Research, was aflame with light when Saxon climbed from the robot cab and approached the entrance. The shadowy figure of a guard challenged him.

Saxon produced his papers, submitted to a fingerprint test.

"So it's you, all right," the guard growled. "Where the hell have you been? The T.I.S. has been scouring the city for you."

Saxon asked, "Is Villainowski in? I want to see him."

"Not half as bad," said the guard, "as he wants to see you." He stuck his head inside the guardroom, yelled, "Hey, Webb, come relieve me. That missing physicist has shown up. I've got to take him up to the chief."

"I can find my way," Saxon assured him dryly.

"I've got my orders," retorted the man, "to escort you, and escorted you'll be."

As they took the lift, Saxon probed gently into the guard's mind. He was thinking about a Venusian dancer performing at the Sun Palace on Greater Broadway. Either he didn't know why Villainowski wanted him, or he was more interested in the dancer.

Saxon sighed in resignation.

Chief Villainowski was a small wiry man of Polish descent who had led none too reputable a life, although it was not generally known. Jon Saxon, regarding him across the polished desk, read suspicion and wonder in the chief's mind. Villainowski was never able to reconcile Saxon's appearance with his indisputable scientific attainments.

"Looks like a plug ugly," Villainowski was thinking although he was far from a beauty himself. *"Ought to be a prize fighter instead of a physicist!"*

"Will you pray tell me," he asked aloud of the amused Saxon, "what the hell possessed you to sneak out the night before we leave?"

Saxon grinned like a mastiff. "It was that General Atomic affair. I haven't told you, but I met one of their agents, a girl by the name of Ileth Urban, about a month ago."

"Redheaded girl?" asked the third man in the room. He had his chair leaned against the wall. A tall, angular, sandy haired man with pale blue eyes like gimlets. "Does she have hazel-green eyes, small delicate features? Ears peaked like an animals..."

"I hadn't noticed the ears," Saxon confessed, swinging toward the sandy-haired man.

Gavin Murdock, T.I.S. agent, had been assigned as T.I.S. representative to this first expedition beyond the Solar System. He said, "No, I guess not. She wears her hair in a page-boy bob."

Villainowski interrupted: "Well, damn it, man, who gave you permission to horn in on the T.I.S.'s work?"

"I knew her. She'd been set to pump me dry of information by General Atomic. If anyone could get anything out of her, I could."

"You don't fancy yourself much," the chief grunted with a touch of asperity. "What did you find out?"

Saxon related events just as they had transpired, omitting only the alien telepaths in the street and his own telepathic ability.

"By Pluto!" exploded Villainowski when he had concluded. "We can grab the lot of them."

"Not so fast," Murdock interrupted from his chair against the wall. "What proof have you? Only Saxon's word. It won't hold in a court of law."

"But the girl!" Villainowski protested. "She's General Atomic's representative on the expedition. You don't intend to let her—"

"It's better to have her where we can watch her," the T.I.S. agent returned. "Saxon can keep an eye on her. He seems to be able to pry more out of her than any of my agents have. If he can persuade her that he hasn't told us about the fracas in her apartment..."

"I can convince her of that, I think," said Saxon. "But she doesn't know anything..."

"Except," Murdock interrupted again, "that she's to take orders from an agent known as Q62. At least, she should lead us to him." He paused, regarded Saxon with his penetrating pale blue eyes. "What the devil did you do to her, man, to get that information out of her? Stick darts under her finger nails?"

In both Murdock's and Villainowski's mind Saxon read a cold determination to keep him under surveillance as well as the girl.

VILLAINOWSKI, he knew, hated the corporations in general, but it was nothing to the black flame of hatred that consumed the man whenever he thought of General Atomic. It was almost psychopathic. He had never forgotten or forgiven General Atomic, Saxon knew, for stealing his first three discoveries and then disgracing him.

It was a queer friendship that existed between the two men questioning Saxon—the gaunt cold-blooded manhunter, who had sent a girl with whom he was infatuated to the Lunar Penal Colony, and Villainowski, the small wiry scientist, ex-Jovian slaver, and at present head of the first expedition into deep space.

"Well," the sandy-haired Murdock repeated inexorably, "how did she happen to tell you about Q62?"

"It was a slip," explained Saxon. "I followed it up."

"She's not given to making slips," Murdock pointed out. "Not Ileth Urban."

When Saxon didn't reply, the T.I.S. agent said, "Saxon, we've investigated your past pretty thoroughly. We did the same with every man and woman connected with this expedition. We encountered a strange thing. Saxon, who are your parents?"

Jon Saxon could feel his stomach contract. "I don't know. I haven't any recollection before my eleventh year." He could feel Murdock's probing blue eyes, sense his skepticism.

"You've a convenient memory, because we've been unable to find any trace of your parents or birth prior to your enrollment in the Institute. A thousand years ago your case would have been unusual, but it could have happened. But today, with our universal system of records, it's impossible. I've never encountered a parallel case to yours."

"I'm sorry," said Saxon dryly, "but I do seem to have been born, don't I? And somehow escaped the census."

Murdock smiled a wintry smile. "There were funds deposited at the Institute for your education. We haven't been able to trace those funds either. In fact, every way we've turned, we've run into a blank wall."

"I'm sorry," said Saxon again, "but I can't help you. I have absolutely no memory before I was eleven. Don't think it hasn't worried me. I asked the T.I.S. to investigate it years ago. They couldn't find anything then. It's not surprising they haven't found anything this time."

"You won't object to being examined by our N.P.A.?"

"No," replied Saxon.

Villainowski spoke into an inter-communicating audio, "Send in the N.P.A."

The neuro-psychoanalyst must have been waiting outside because he entered immediately. Saxon regarded him curiously. Government's N.P.A. was a lean Cassius-like individual with an ingratiating smile. Saxon had taken an immediate dislike to him when he had first seen him prowling about the corridors of the research building, but he knew the man was a brilliant psychologist.

The N.P.A. approached Saxon rubbing his hands together and smiling. "So this is the subject. How are you, Jon? There's no need to ask questions. I've studied your record. No question but what there's a mental block, is there? Hope we can break it. Sit here, if you don't mind."

Saxon took the chair indicated, the N.P.A. facing him.

"Take one of these." He held out a box of hypno-pills.

Saxon selected one, gulped it down. He made no effort to read the minds of Murdock, Villainowski or the N.P.A.

The neuro-psychoanalyst was wearing a revolving mirror about an inch in diameter on a band about his forehead. He set the mirror in motion, which caught the room light, alternately, darkening and flashing.

"Look into the light, Jon," he said in a calm, sure voice. "Relax and watch the light. You are going to sleep when I count three. You can feel the effect of the hypno-pill already. When I count three you sleep, sleep...One." A pause. "Two." Pause. "Three..."

AFTER half an hour the N.P.A.'s voice wasn't so sure. He had given Jon three more pills, had tried all the devices at the command of the largest neural-clinic in the Empire without the slightest effect. Jon Saxon continued to regard the N.P.A. with a half-hidden gleam of amusement in his dark gray eyes.

The neuro-psychoanalyst sat back, mopped his perspiring face with his handkerchief. "It's no use," he said in a strained voice. "He can't be hypnotized!"

"I could have told you that," replied Saxon. "Do you think I haven't tried to have the block broken before?"

The N.P.A. swore and got to his feet. "Well, why didn't you say so?" he shouted. It was the first time Saxon had ever seen him lose his temper.

"Because these gentlemen have been suspicious of me." He indicated Murdock and Villainowski. "If I had offered any objections to being hypnotized, they'd have been sure that I was afraid to."

All at once, Saxon experienced the peculiar tingling in scalp and skin that warned him the alien creatures, which he had met in the street, were present. He couldn't possibly be mistaken. Once having experienced that peculiar inhuman feel it was not to be forgotten or confused.

Not only were they invisible, but neither doors nor walls seemed to offer any resistance to them.

"Who are you?" he concentrated, but his thought met that strange mental barrier. There was no answer.

He realized that the three men were watching him with a curious tenseness.

Suddenly the N.P.A.'s jaw dropped. An expression of complete astonishment lit up his face. "I've got it! I've got it!" he cried.

"Got what?" growled Villainowski, moving uneasily behind his massive desk.

"Saxon! Saxon, that's who! My Lord, why didn't it occur to me before. He's a—"

The words died suddenly on the N.P.A.'s lips. An expression of fright crossed his lean features. Then, without a sound, he crumpled to the carpet.

Jon Saxon, staring in horror, realized that the tingling of his skin was diminishing. The telepaths were withdrawing.

At the same instant Murdock's chair hit the floor as he leaped across the room, dropped to his knee beside the prone figure of the N.P.A. For a moment he was bent over the body like a bronze statue, then he turned his face up to Villainowski.

Saxon, who had read his thoughts, was amazed at Murdock's passionless expression.

"He's dead," the T.I.S. agent said in a toneless voice. "I wouldn't have believed it, if I hadn't seen it happen, but he's deader than the moon."

CHAPTER FOUR

BONG! BONG! BONG! BONG! rang the warning gong, reverberating through the launching pit.

Mustapha IX had shaken hands for the last time with Villainowski and hurried down the gangplank. The ports were all sealed; crew at their stations. Outside the pits, the frenzied crowd was delirious with excitement. Wasn't it man's first attempt to reach the stars?

Bong! Bong! Bong! Bong! Bong!

On the last stroke the *Shooting Star* fell silent except for the muffled roar of her tubes warming. At the same instant the crowd grew impossibly still.

The raw fear, which had made itself felt in spite of the festivities, rode to the surface. The strange psychological dread of deep space.

A woman in the relatives' stand suddenly buried her face in her hands, her shoulders shaking with violent sobs. She was the wife of the master mechanic on the third's watch. A gray-faced man moved towards the woman, patted her shoulders.

Just then a continuous violent explosion shook the frail stand like an earth tremor. The *Shooting Star* burst from the pits, trailing a comet-tail of orange flame.

"Oh, my husband!" wailed the woman, "oh, my husband!" but her voice was drowned in the roar.

JON SAXON threw off his safety belt, glanced across at the strained white face of Ileth Urban in the next acceleration chair. "Buck up," he grinned. "It's too late to change your mind now."

The girl nervously tucked a curl in place, smiled uncertainly. "Heaven help me! Are we going to share all my thoughts during the rest of the voyage?"

"Hell, no," said Saxon. "I want to preserve some of my illusions." He leaned towards her. "I'll strike a bargain with you, though. If you don't mention that I'm a telepath, I'll not report our—er—experience last night."

"You mean you haven't said anything?"

"No," said Saxon. "Why should I? I didn't have proof. Who'd want to tackle General Atomic without cast-iron evidence? On second thought, who'd want to tackle General Atomic at all? No one would believe me, anyway. Just like they won't believe you if you tell them I'm a telepath."

Saxon could see the girl reach a decision. "Oh, I wouldn't say that," he broke in before she could voice her thought. "You've lots of other courses. You could snub me or spread tales behind my back."

"I didn't say it!" she retorted hotly. "I thought it. My Lord, I can't even call my thoughts my own!"

"Then it's a bargain."

"I didn't say so."

"No. But you've decided to…"

She stamped her feet. "That's what I mean! That's what I mean!"

"Calm down," he said. "Half the staff is staring at you."

Ileth drew a deep breath, shrugged. A grim smile flashed across her pretty patrician features.

"If you can stand it," she replied with an unexpected twinkle in her hazel-green eyes, "I suppose I can too."

He stood up. "Like to meet the rest of the staff? Fine. You're all settled in your cabin, aren't you? No? Then I'll give you a hand as soon as we finish our tour of introduction."

Ileth's eyes had grown darker and darker.

"Now don't lose your temper," he said hastily.

"I haven't said a damn word. At least let me get my answers out of my mouth."

Saxon laughed, taking her arm. "Come along. We're accelerating at one-G constant. We'll have no trouble moving around." He hesitated, then asked in an off hand manner.

"Has Q62 identified himself yet?"

Ileth looked startled, frightened. She tried to draw away but Saxon held onto her arm. "No. No, he hasn't. Please let go. You're hurting me, Jon."

But he didn't release her. "Is he aboard the ship?"

"No. I don't know. General Atomic didn't notify me that he would be." Abruptly, Ileth didn't seem confused any longer. She raised her chin, looked Saxon nakedly in the eyes making no effort to conceal her thoughts. "I think he is," she said simply. "But I don't know. He hasn't identified himself, if he is. I—I haven't seen anyone aboard that I know. I think I'm the only General Atomic agent aboard, and I'm an accredited representative."

Saxon regarded her a moment without speaking. The girl was telling the truth as far as she knew. There could be no doubt about that.

SAXON introduced Ileth to Brand, Government's biochemist, to Mercedes, the gray-haired middle-aged woman who was Government's authority in anthropology. He made the circuit of the lounge with her, letting her chat with ethnologists and semantics experts, psycho-historians and zoologists—all of Government's brilliant array of specialists. And all the while he kept his mind open and alert, sifting their varied thought patterns for a betraying sign.

He didn't intercept a single suspicious thought.

They all seemed to be just exactly what they were supposed to be, each one an expert in his field, eager and enthusiastic investigators beginning an unparalleled adventure. Saxon could discover no evidences that any of them had sold out to General Atomic.

If Q62 or any General Atomic agent were among Government's staff, they were perfect in dissembling their thoughts.

From the lounge, Saxon showed Ileth about the ship. He could see it was an experience for the girl.

The *Shooting Star* had been built along the general design of a cruiser, heavily armed and armored against the possibilities of hostile races inhabiting the planets of the Alpha Centaurian suns.

Her crew was small. Government's staff of scientists numbered fourteen; and only four of the corporations were represented: General Atomic, Tri-World, Amalgamated Plastic and United Spaceways. In spite of the mass of equipment and a year's emergency ration of fuel and supplies, they were not crowded.

Saxon led Ileth through the control room, the officer's mess, the engine room and observation deck. Everywhere they went, Saxon probed the brains of crew and officers.

At the end of two hours, he still had found exactly nothing. Apparently Q62 was not aboard. Ileth asked slyly, "Did you find him?"

They had entered the deck on which the cabins were located and were passing the closed door of number seven.

"Q62?" said Saxon with a puzzled frown. "No—" He halted abruptly, seizing the girl's arm.

"Jon! What is it?"

"Be quiet!"

Saxon's scalp was tingling as if minute electrical shocks were coursing through the roots of his hair.

The Aliens?

The feel was unmistakable to his extra-human sixth sense. And it was emanating from Cabin Seven!

Like a cat he reached the door in one silent bound, pressed the button. The panel slid back noiselessly. Except for a blade of light lancing into the cabin from the lighted passage, only darkness lurked beyond the doorway.

The alien inhuman feel was suddenly so strong that it was like a cold draft pouring through the blackened entrance, sending chills rippling up his spine.

Ileth's eyes were enormous. Saxon could hear her frightened erratic breathing. Her fear-thoughts beat at his brain. *"What is it? What has he found? What's wrong?"*

In spite of himself, Saxon could feel the blood drain out of his cheeks. He wanted suddenly to slam the door and run blindly down the corridor, away from that strange creature lurking in the dark of Cabin Seven.

He controlled himself, reached noiselessly inside the door, pressed the switch. Light flooded the cabin.

"Why, it's just a girl!" said Ileth, who was peering wide-eyed over Saxon's shoulder. She giggled nervously.

Saxon stared at the occupant of the cabin, scarcely crediting his eyes. It was a girl right enough, a flaxen haired girl sleeping easily on her back in the narrow bunk.

A thin flexoplas coverlet was thrown across her. One slim bare leg dangled over the edge of the bunk. Her face, Saxon saw, was heart shaped, the closed eyelids delicately blue.

At Ileth's giggle, the creature opened her eyes, sat upright with a half-suppressed scream. Ileth backed out of the doorway in embarrassment, but Saxon stood as if turned to stone.

The tingling sensation was sending goose flesh racing over his skin. The alien emanations were streaming straight from the girl on the bunk.

He recovered himself, thought violently, angrily, *"Who are you?"*

The girl stared at him without making a sound. Saxon realized that her eyes were amber as topaz, large and strangely lambent. Then a faint smile twitched the corners of her lips. She made no move to escape, not even to cover her breasts and shoulder.

"You!" the thought reached Saxon tinged with amusement. *"It would be you who discovered me!"*

She touched a tiny instrument strapped to her wrist, which Saxon noticed for the first time.

"Who are you?" he thought again, then narrowed his eyes with crazed disbelief.

He could see the bulkhead through the girl. She gave a low laugh. The flexoplas coverlet, which had lain so lightly over her lap, collapsed slowly.

The girl was gone, dissolved. Only her throaty laugh lingered in the still air.

Saxon rubbed his eyes. He felt Ileth trembling against him as if she had a chill. Setting his jaw, he stepped up to the bunk, felt the sheets. They were warm and still held the impression of the girl's body.

He straightened, realized that the tingling in his scalp had ceased. The alien telepath was gone. But where?

"Let's get the hell out of here," Ileth said vehemently.

Saxon followed her into the passage, switched off the lights, closed the door softly behind him.

"I don't believe it!" said Ileth. "I don't want to believe it." Her fine patrician features were paper white, making her dark lashes and eyebrows stand out like heavy strokes of a crayon. Her lips were bloodless.

Saxon shook his head in bewilderment.

"Couldn't you read her mind?" asked Ileth.

"She had the most perfect mental barrier I've ever encountered. I couldn't read a thing. Only…"

"Only what?"

"Nothing," he said abruptly, shaking his massive shoulders as if to free them from a burden. "Nothing. I think we'd better keep our mouths shut about this too. If we went around telling what we've seen, they'd throw us in the psychopathic ward."

Ileth shuddered.

"Maybe it was an hallucination," she suggested. "Maybe we're nutty as a fruit cake, I hope."

CHAPTER FIVE

YOU'VE BEEN THROUGH THE Little Death before,"
said Saxon. He and Murdock, the T.I.S. agent, were in the
control room, Murdock's eye glued to the scanner. "What's it
like, Murdock?"

The gaunt, frosty T.I.S. agent took his eyes from the
scanner, faced Saxon.

"Not so bad," he replied laconically.

"I've heard it's a pretty rugged experience."

Murdock allowed himself a tight smile.

"That depends on how active a social consciousness you
have. You're a non-Newtonian physicist. You know the
Pachner conception of the space-time continuum better than
I do. Villainowski's stellar drive inverts the Newtonian
concept that a vehicle travels through space during a passage
of time. It operates through time during a passage of space.

"Yes, yes," Saxon interrupted impatiently. "But the effects
of the time field... What do you experience while the ship is
in the time field?"

"That's the Little Death," replied Murdock in a dry voice,
"though the name is misleading. Actually you experience a
segment of your own life, either the past, the future, or the
present. As Villainowski would explain it, time is co-existent,
while in the time field our lives are spread out around us, but
because we're equipped with three dimensional sense organs
we're restricted to a single series of episodes anywhere along
our life span."

Saxon frowned and said, "In other words, it's just as if we
returned to the past and relived some incident that occurred
to us before?"

"Right. Or into the future and experienced something that hasn't happened yet."

Saxon's frown deepened. "But what's so rugged about that?"

"Nothing," rejoined Murdock dryly, "if you've lived an exemplary life. It's not pleasant, though, to live over and over again a period when you committed murder say, or were terribly frightened, or even did some little thing that you've been trying your best to forget since."

Saxon caught a brief mental flash from the T.I.S. agent, as he shoved the picture of a girl with pretty Slavic features out of his mind.

"I'm not looking forward to the Little Death!" Murdock said dryly, and returned his eye to the scanner.

Saxon leaned back in the acceleration chair. The captain was bending over the three-dimensional space-charts along with the third mate. A spaceman stood at the robot pilot. Another, whom Murdock had replaced at the scanner, was reclining in a second acceleration chair.

There was an air of tension in the control room. Saxon realized suddenly that the captain was checking the robot controls.

That could mean only one thing. It was nearing time for Villainowski to switch the *Shooting Star* onto the stellar drive. They would be going into the Little Death any moment. Saxon sat up abruptly. "How long before we switch over, Captain?"

The captain looked up from the charts. "We've attained minimum velocity. Villainowski's in the engine room now. I'm expecting orders to turn her over right away."

Murdock turned from the scanner again, fixed Saxon with his pale blue eyes.

"By the way, Jon, you've been prowling the ship from stem to stern the past three days." His voice was pitched too

THE OUTCASTS OF SOLAR III

low to reach the officers checking the star maps and robot controls. "Have you a line on Q62 yet?"

Saxon could read suspicion in the T.I.S. agent's mind. "No," he admitted, "and I'm more puzzled than you. Ileth doesn't know who Q62 is, or even if he's aboard, although she's been commanded by General Atomic to take her orders from him."

"You're sure of that?"

"Yes. I'm sure of it."

There was a pause, each man busy with his own thoughts.

"I'd swear," Saxon broke the silence, "that Q62 isn't aboard, nor any other General Atomic agents."

Murdock regarded him speculatively and Saxon caught his thought, *"What the hell makes him so damned sure?"*

SURE? Saxon thought to himself. He wasn't sure about anything. The alien stowaway was still aboard. His sixth sense had warned him of her nearness a hundred times during his sporadic jaunts about the ship. But he had been unable to establish contact with her.

He had kept his mind open to the wash of thoughts from crew and staff, but, so far as he had been able to learn, they were all loyal to Government. Not even in their secret innermost thoughts had he discovered any evidence that a traitor was aboard.

Murdock interrupted his reflections, asking, "Have you any idea what that N.P.A. had discovered before he died?"

Saxon started, looked at the T.I.S. agent uncomfortably. Murdock's irrelevant question had conjured a vivid picture in his mind of the death of the N.P.A. in Villainowski's office.

"I don't know," he said miserably, beginning to understand how uncomfortable the Little Death might be. "I would give a lot to know. He may have had a clue to what I am."

Murdock's cold blue eyes narrowed, and he regarded Saxon with a peculiar intensity. *"That's a devilish odd way for him to put it,"* the T.I.S. agent was thinking. *"What he is! Now why the hell would he say that?"*

Saxon realized with chagrin that he had made a slip. He should have said, "Who I am," not "What I am." No human ever doubted that he was a genuine specimen of *homo sapiens.*

The engine room telegraph buzzed suddenly, and when the captain answered, Villainowski's voice reached the two men.

"Sound the general alarm, Captain. Turn the ship over to the robot control. We're going into the Little Death."

"Right," said the captain. He looked pale and worn and older. He snapped off the telegraph, turned to the third. "Sound the general alarm and turn on the public address system, then go to your cabin." The third nodded, reached for the switch.

An ugly clangor broke through the *Shooting Star* from stem to stern, followed immediately by a harsh metallic voice issuing from strategically placed audios.

"All officers, members of unlicensed personnel and staff report to your quarters at once and lie on your bunks."

There was a series of clicks as the ship went smoothly over to the robot controls.

The command ordering everyone to their cabins was repeated three more times.

Saxon realized there was no one in the control room, but himself, Murdock, and the captain.

"Coming?" asked the captain from the doorway.

"In a minute," Murdock replied.

The captain departed hastily, and Saxon followed the T.I.S. agent across the deck to the control board, where a single dial was marked off in parsecs.

"I'm damned curious about this four-dimensional drive," Murdock confessed, as he dropped into an acceleration chair before the dial. "I've been through it before. But I'd like to follow its operation here in the control room as long as possible before we blank out. Are you game?"

"Sure," Saxon's voice was eager. He took a seat beside Murdock, staring at the dial marked off in parsecs with fascination.

He became conscious of a sobering silence. The robot controls had cut off the jets. A giddy feeling of weightlessness possessed him.

Suddenly the radiograph began to click off a message. He saw Murdock frown, tear off the tape, read it.

"Good Lord!" the T.I.S. agent burst out. "Read it! We've got to get to Villainowski before we go onto the stellar drive!" He leaped to his feet, went soaring in the air, a pained expression on his face. Murdock had forgotten their weightless condition now that the jets were off.

Saxon who had snatched the strip of paper, flashed his eye over the words.

IMPERIAL HEADQUARTERS:
TO CHIEF J. VILLAINOWSKI. URGENT. ORDERS CANCELLED. TURN BACK TO EARTH WITHOUT DELAY. ALL FIVE COPIES OF STEL-LAR DRIVE STOLEN. GOVERNMENT CANNOT RISK YOUR LIFE IN DEEP SPACE UNTIL YOU CAN REPLACE PLANS.

MUSTAPHA IX.

Saxon realized the machine was still clicking off the message over and over again.

Murdock had pushed himself to the bulkhead, where he kicked off, gliding through the door. Saxon followed cautiously, conscious of a yellow mist collecting in the control room.

The T.I.S. agent got just beyond the doorway when he floated unconscious to the deck.

Saxon made it to the head of the ladder. Then he, too, lost control over his muscles.

The mist was like soup, thick yellow pea soup.

His last conscious thought was, "So this is the Little Death!"

HERE! Why are you crying?" asked the big white giant. His voice was gentle, compassionate, and he was naked except for a kilt of a strange gleaming material like woven light.

"But I don't want to go," Saxon protested in a reedy, childish tone. He realized in dismay that the giant wasn't a giant at all, but normal and man-sized. "I don't want to go," he heard himself tearfully repeating.

They were in a room, the little boy that had been Saxon and the big white man, and a door across the room was opening. The little boy that was Saxon shrank against the man.

A woman appeared in the doorway. She was tall and beautiful and dressed like the man in a gleaming kilt. She smiled at Saxon, but he was not reassured. He hung back from crossing the threshold.

Saxon saw a troubled look pass between the two. Then the man steeled himself, picked up the squirming boy, carried him through the doorway.

It was a strange sensation that possessed the mature Saxon, stretched on the cold deck at the head of the ladder to the engine room. He wasn't dreaming. He was the little boy, and yet he seemed to be outside himself, watching his own actions, appraising himself like the detached half of a dual personality.

He was in the time field, Saxon realized. That was it! He was reliving a segment of his life span that had taken place before he was eleven!

His heart leaped spasmodically. At last the curtain was being raised on those blank years of childhood!

The room into which the man carried him, Saxon saw, was larger than the anteroom and cluttered with strange machinery, ugly machinery. The far wall was a solid bank of windows, through which he could see a green meadow rolling gently away to blue foothills in the distance. Light poured through the windows from a blazing sun high overhead and a second orange sun was just rising.

The man deposited him in a chair. Saxon quit thrashing, as the woman fitted a skullcap over his head, making minute adjustments. A cable led from the peak of the skullcap to a frightening machine which the woman bent over next, and set in operation.

Saxon could feel a rush of thought pouring into his brain. Queer thoughts couched in semantically obscure words.

One stood out. *"Earth."* It was repeated many times before he began to comprehend the import of the alien symbols. *"Earth is the third planet of a star known to its inhabitants as Sol."*

With a feeling of strangeness the Saxon who observed realized that the boy was being taught to speak English!

SAXON shook his head groggily, pushed himself to his hands and knees and found himself floating six feet in the air. He had forgotten that the jet drive was still off.

It came back with a suddenness that flung Saxon to the metal deck.

He scrambled to his feet, his mind in a whirl. Forgotten temporarily were the emergency orders commanding them to return to Earth. If Villainowski had been right, then Saxon had actually relived an event, which had transpired before he was eleven.

Then who the hell was he?

He returned to the control room, stepping over the unconscious body of Murdock, who had not yet recovered from the effects of the time field.

The dial on the control board read 1.3 parsecs!

He jumped for the scanner, clamped his eye to the aperture, and immediately jumped back!

Dead ahead was a huge blazing sun!

It looked so close that the *Shooting Star* appeared to be falling straight into the maw of erupting atomic energy.

But reason returned, and he knew they were still millions of miles away. He went to the scanner, spotting first a second sun not so close, then a third, small and red like a fiery coin.

The ternary system of Alpha Centauri! They were out of the Solar System!

"Please," said a girl's voice behind him. "Stand back from the scanner! Don't try for your gun, Saxon, or I will be forced to shoot!"

Saxon whirled around.

Ileth Urban stood in the doorway, a dart gun leveled at his stomach. Behind her, he saw the shame-faced Murdock surrounded by the crew. Murdock was helpless, his arms in the air.

"The crew have mutinied," said Ileth. "The ship is now under the control of General Atomic."

Saxon's jaw sagged. He said, "So you are Q62." It wasn't so much a question as a statement. He knew. He read it in her thoughts. But why hadn't he seen it there before?

It wasn't possible, but there could be no doubt. Ileth Urban was Q62.

Then the thoughts of the men in the corridor made themselves felt. Every man jack of them had gone over to General Atomic, not recently, but weeks and months ago, before they had ever left Earth.

He dropped into a chair, his head in his hands. How had they been able to disguise their thoughts all this time?

He looked at Ileth in her chartreuse green short-waisted jacket. She held the dart gun leveled at his chest. Her patrician features were set in grim unhappy lines.

"Something!" Saxon thought wildly. "Something has gone terribly wrong!"

CHAPTER SIX

THE T.I.S. AGENT, HIS BONY fingers locked beneath his head, was stretched face up on his bunk. There were five of them in the ship's brig—Saxon, Murdock and Villainowski, Mercedes, the anthropologist and Brand, the biochemist.

"Jon, that girl's crazy about you."

"What?" Jon Saxon swung up his head, regarded Murdock coldly.

Without moving, the T.I.S. agent repeated, "She's in love with you, Jon. Though what Ileth can find to love in that ugly granite mug of yours is beyond comprehension."

Saxon said, "So what?" Everyone was watching him speculatively.

They had been cooped together for nine days now, the four men and the woman. Yesterday the ship had landed. But none of them knew where.

"So what?" Murdock echoed breaking the silence. "My Lord, man, play up to her. She's eating her heart out for you. Can't you see it's our only chance?"

"No," said Saxon stiffly and blocked out their thoughts. "No, I don't. You know as well as I do, that the crew and the officers, even the staff, except Mercedes and Brand here sold out to General Atomic. Suppose I did persuade Ileth to let us out. Suppose she comes over to our side—which I tell you right now she won't—but suppose she did. What possible chance would the five of us have against sixty armed desperate men and women? Hell, Murdock, we couldn't even get the ship back to Earth by ourselves!" He hesitated. "Besides it strikes me as a contemptible stunt..."

Murdock's cold blue eyes flashed. He sat up, swinging his feet to the deck. "Do you think we're playing a game?"

Mercedes, the gray-haired woman, interrupted, "Don't nag him, Murdock. Everyone isn't a cold-blooded monster like you."

The T.I.S. agent grunted his disgust, lay back down and rolled to his stomach.

Mercedes was a pleasant-faced, middle-aged woman with bright black eyes like a parrot.

"I don't see yet," she continued imperturbably, "how General Atomic could contact everyone before we sailed." She smoothed her skirts, sitting primly on the brig's only chair, and cast a sly look at Murdock. "Not with the vaunted T.I.S. on guard."

"Humph!" came Murdock's muffled voice from the pillow. "What's so damned impossible about that? We couldn't watch the beggars all the time." He rolled back and sat up again.

"No. What bothers me is why they didn't give themselves away. They were investigated. All of them were reputable Government men, their fathers Government men before 'em."

"It's hard to refuse a million credits," Saxon pointed out.

Murdock's pale blue eyes jerked to Saxon. "How do you know?"

Before Saxon could reply, Mercedes said, "General Atomic offered us all a million credits. They did to me and Brand, I know. We reported it to the T.I.S."

"Yeah," said Murdock with a frown. "Yeah, and we questioned them with the lie-detector. Not once, but every time they left the building. They were psychoanalyzed and searched. And every damned one of them was certified loyal to Government. They never gave a sign that they'd sold out to General Atomic, not a sign. Why, the bums acted as if they didn't know it themselves."

"They didn't!" put in Saxon.

Their eyes swung back to the burly nuclear physicist. He read skepticism, doubt, curiosity in their minds.

"What do you mean?" Murdock exploded.

"I mean just what I said. They actually didn't know that they had sold out to General Atomic until after the Little Death. It's simple enough. I'm surprised no one's thought of it before. Ever since Charcot back in the nineteenth century..."

"Hypnotism!" Villainowski burst out. "That's it, of course! Post-hypnotic commands!"

Saxon nodded. "I wasn't sure. I'm not sure even yet." But he was. He had known it the moment he had looked into Ileth's mind the day of the mutiny.

Murdock frowned, said, "Post-hypnotic commands? I don't follow you."

"There's nothing mysterious about it, actually," explained Saxon. "When the men sold out to General Atomic they must have submitted to being hypnotized by GA's neuro-psychoanalyst. They could be given orders while in the hypnotic state, then commanded to forget them, forget in fact that they had sold out to General Atomic until after the Little Death. The Little Death was to act as a post-hypnotic command, recalling their memories and instructions."

"By Pluto!" ejaculated Murdock. "I believe you've hit it!" He regarded Saxon with increased respect.

The slight, homely Villainowski rubbed a nine-day's growth of beard, musing, "It was a beautiful scheme. Then men couldn't betray themselves. They couldn't be tripped up by the lie-detector because they honestly believed they were still loyal to Government."

Again Saxon nodded. "I was trying to find Q62," he said, "when Ileth was Q62 all the time, although she didn't know it until she woke up from the Little Death."

BRAND, the biochemist, who had been lying on an upper bunk silently listening, broke into the conversation. "But why did General Atomic wait until after the Little Death before having their men seize the ship? It doesn't make sense. I should think they'd want to get the drive to one of their laboratories, where it could be examined as soon as possible."

It was Murdock who replied. "That's not difficult to explain either. General Atomic couldn't afford to take a chance. If they'd grabbed the *Shooting Star* within reach of Government's space navy, they would have been apprehended sure. Remember, every observatory in the System had us in view until we went into the time field.

"No one but Villainowski knows how to use the stellar drive, so they couldn't have used that to escape. But after we reached Alpha Centauri we were beyond reach of the electronic telescope on Luna, even beyond radio contact. Their engineers would have a chance to examine the drive and learn enough to operate it, at least. They could return then. Nothing can catch the *Shooting Star* when she's operating in the Little Death."

Saxon listened with somber eyes to the T.I.S. agent's explanation. It was right, he felt, as far as it went. But it didn't account for the aliens, or for Saxon's strange experiences during the Little Death, or the death of that N.P.A. before they sailed.

He heard the door to the brig click and glanced up just as it slid aside.

Ileth Urban stood in the entrance.

Ileth's green jodhpur-like trousers emphasized her long legs and slim waist. Her shoulder length hair had been pushed back, disclosing small peaked ears.

She came inside, with a look of determination, and the guard closed the door behind her, but didn't lock it.

"I..." she began, caught Saxon's eyes and blushed furiously. Unconsciously her chin went up and she squared her shoulders. "I don't know how to say what I've come to tell you." Again she hesitated, biting her lip. "I think it'll be good news..."

"Good news?" echoed Murdock sarcastically. "Have the crew been massacred by Centaurians?"

"There's no sign of living Centaurians yet," she replied. "Not on this planet anyway."

"Living Centaurians?" asked Murdock. "What do you mean 'living' Centaurians? What have you found?"

The silence was alive. Saxon could feel the intangible fear of deep space grip every one of them. There was, he realized, a decided pathologic quality about it, as if every one of them were not quite sane on the subject.

"A city," said Ileth is a suppressed voice.

There was a quick intake of breaths. "Yes," she went on, "a city. About twenty-five kilometers northeast of here. A perfectly huge city without a single inhabitant."

"What planet is this?" Villainowski asked suddenly.

"There's no harm in telling you, I suppose," said Ileth. "Because we haven't the faintest notion. Our astronomer says that it belongs to Alpha Centauri A, although he hasn't figured its period yet. He says it's about midway between Alpha Centauri A and Alpha Centauri B. It's a little larger than Earth but not so dense. Gravity is about four fifths what it is at home." Her face sobered at the word 'home.' "Oxygen content a little high, but not much. The rest of the atmosphere is composed principally of non-poisonous inert gases. Now you know as much as we do."

Jon Saxon became aware of a thought emanating from Murdock: *"Seize the girl. Dictate terms to the others."* The same though, Saxon realized, was forming in their biochemist's mind as well.

Ileth must have suspected something, because her hand crept up to her small high breasts and she said, "Before I go on, you'd better know that I'm not so unprotected as I look. We were all hypnotized back on Earth and our orders given to us in that condition. Then we were commanded to forget them until after the Little Death. I'm telling you this so you'll understand."

The prisoners exchanged glances.

"General Atomic," Ileth continued hurriedly, "prepared for any eventuality. If anything happens to me, Q63 will take over. I don't know who he is, and he doesn't know it himself, but any accident befalling me will be the post-hypnotic signal for him to remember. There's also a Q64, Q65—all the way to Q70. So you see it's useless to think that by doing anything to me you can get the upper hand."

"Rather like queen bees," suggested Saxon. "Secret order with a vengeance."

"Even from you, darling!" he caught Ileth's irritating thought.

HE SAW Murdock relax on his bunk, intercepted his furious frustration. The T.I.S. agent, he realized, was like cold flame on the inside.

"But that's not my news," Ileth said. "I've come to offer you your freedom—within limits, of course."

"Eh?" said Villainowski in surprise, and the rest tensed expectantly.

Ileth said, "General Atomic believed that it would be to their advantage to go ahead with the expedition as soon as we got control of the ship. We would be on the spot, and any information relating to Alpha Centauri's planetary systems, natural resources, inhabitants (if any), possibilities of colonization and trade—that sort of thing—is of the utmost importance.

"I feel..." She hesitated, and Saxon caught a glimpse again of that same intolerable fear gnawing at her mind.

"I feel that we should stick together—while we're here at least. If we're fighting among ourselves..."

"In other words," Murdock interrupted in a voice without inflection, "you're asking us to go on with the expedition as if nothing's happened?"

"Only while we're here," she hastened to assure him. "You won't be given arms, of course. There are only five of you. What earthly chance would you have against the entire crew and the rest of the staff? And this way you won't have to stay locked in the brig. You can carry on with your investigations. We—we don't know what alien form of life inhabits this planet. But the city..."

She bit her lip again. "The city was peculiar."

A short uncomfortable silence greeted her statement; then Mercedes, the gray-haired anthropologist asked, "What do you mean, child?"

"I don't know how to define it. Wait until you see it."

But Saxon had intercepted an image in Ileth's mind—a distorted glimpse of a vast beautiful city stretching for kilometer after kilometer without a soul anywhere. A sobering chill prickled up his spine. He said, "I, for my part, am willing to call a truce, Ileth."

The girl glanced at him gratefully. Saxon became aware of a passionate thought: *Oh, the darling stiff-necked bear!* The girl's color heightened suddenly. She began to think furiously: *Two times two is four; three times two is six; four times two is eight...*

Saxon grinned at her knowingly, to her added confusion.

"I hate you!" she thought.

Villainowski jumped to his feet, saying, "Of course we accept. We all accept. But let me warn you, young woman, aliens or no aliens, I don't care if we spend the rest of our lives in the Centaurian system, I'm not going to explain my stellar drive to your scoundrels!"

Ileth turned to him almost gratefully. "Oh, that doesn't matter. Our engineers are examining it. They've assured me that they can take us back to Earth."

Villainowski looked crestfallen.

"Tomorrow," said Ileth in a firm voice, "we're starting to investigate the city. Mercedes is the anthropologist. I particularly wanted her and Saxon along."

"What about the rest of us?" Brand the biochemist, asked.

Ileth ticked them off on her fingers. "Dr. Villainowski is an astro-physicist, I believe. We have the telescope mounted. He and our men are to locate any other planets in the system. You, Dr. Brand, are to go with Loar, the Martian, on an expedition into the hills to the south. Mr. Murdock will be stationed temporarily with the emergency crew aboard the *Shooting Star.*"

Saxon realized that she had cleverly separated them. At the same moment he recognized that leap of fear in Ileth whenever she thought about outside. It was pathologic.

"My Lord!" he thought, "was their fear of deep space driving them insane?"

Ileth was saying, "You can have your old cabins back. I won't see you again until tomorrow. We—we're still on Earth time because of the peculiar daylight hours. Until tomorrow."

She turned, head bent and hurried abruptly through the door.

The prisoners looked at each other in vague alarm, unconsciously drawing closer together. In each of their minds, Saxon read the same thing—the blind unspoken terror of deep space!

THE helicopter whispered scarcely a hundred feet above the rolling plain, while Saxon stared hungrily out of the windows, unable to satisfy his eyes.

Alpha Centauri A, a scintillating yellow orb like Sol, stood in mid-sky. The orange disc that was Alpha Centauri B, the second half of the binary, was just rising. Proxima was not in sight.

Directly below he could see a flock of plants that looked like tumbleweeds except that they were a weirdly mottled yellow and green. They rolled along in a herd pausing to nibble at new shoots of the pale green grass. "Cannibal Plants," their botanist had named them because of their feeding habits.

Herbivorous plants!

Their botanist, Saxon thought, was going quietly insane trying to classify the staggering complexity of utterly alien forms of plant growth.

"Weird, isn't it?" A woman's rich husky voice addressed Saxon. "It sends goose flesh up my spine." Saxon tore his eyes away from the window.

The person sitting beside him was Clo-Javel, a black-eyed woman with cadmium-yellow hair. There was a sleek disturbing fullness to her breasts and hips that was echoed in her red lips and magnificent eyes. She must be thirty-five but no one except possibly the T.I.S. knew her exact age.

Clo-Javel's first passion was archaeology, Saxon knew. Her second was men. He asked, "How many pieces of silver did General Atomic give you?"

Clo-Javel regarded him with an amused tolerant smile. "Don't be rude, Jon."

Saxon, looking into the woman's mind, realized that his thrust hadn't disturbed her in the least. Clo-Javel apparently had no more honor than morals.

There was no question, though, about her archaeological ability. Her reconstruction of the New York skyscrapers, which had perished early in the Atom Age, were famous.

Saxon was appalled. He had expected to uncover a sense of shame among the crew and staff for their treachery. But, if they felt any remorse, they never let it rise into the realms of conscious thought. He had probed their minds one after another, his hope of persuading some of them to return to the Government fold diminished with each one.

At one stroke they had received wealth and better positions with General Atomic's research bureau. They were determined not to lose them. Furthermore, to a man they were convinced that General Atomic would be the next government.

He glanced about the cabin. There were nine of them accompanying Ileth to the deserted city. He allowed their thoughts to wash across his mind, eager, excited, fearful thoughts like half-spoken words.

"Look !" Ileth cried suddenly and pointed ahead. She was piloting the helicopter and spoke over her shoulder. "Look! There's the city!"

Saxon saw a maze of towers scintillating like jewels in the combined light of the twin suns. He saw endless avenues and squares and parks. It was all bright and raw like a city seen in a shimmering mirage.

He swallowed a lump in his throat. He felt… Why, damn it, he felt as if he were coming home after a long time.

Home?

He thought suddenly of his extra-human senses. Maybe this was home! Could it be that he was not of Earth at all? Not a mutant of whom his parents had been ashamed and who had deserted him at the Institute, as he had always believed?

Then Ileth was dropping the helicopter safely into a beautiful square ringed with vari-colored translucent buildings.

Nothing moved. Not the faintest echo of a sound reached Saxon's ears. He found himself holding his breath as the 'copter landed with a faint jar.

Saxon's scalp began to prickle warningly, and such a feel of alienism swept over him, exciting his extra-human sixth sense that he felt giddy.

The city wasn't deserted. It was densely populated.

All around him, everywhere, were aliens. He could sense their movements along the streets, inside the buildings. Hundreds of them.

He heard Ileth's strangely chastened voice. "It's so uncannily deserted. No one. Absolutely no one. What do you suppose happened to the—the things who built this city?"

Saxon had to clench his jaw to keep from shouting, "They're here! You fools, let's get away while we've still got a chance! They're all around us!"

Instead, he kept silent, little beads of perspiration breaking through his prickling skin.

CHAPTER SEVEN

JON SAXON WAS THE FIRST man out of the helicopter. He stood stock-still while the others climbed out, his scalp tingling, his eyes sweeping the magnificent panorama. The faces of buildings like the sheer fracture of tinted ice walled in the square, with here and there a canyon street slicing off from it.

Ileth scrambled out last, asked, "Jon, what's wrong? You're pale as a ghost."

"I don't know." The tingling in his hair roots was becoming less pronounced as his extra-human sixth sense adjusted. He was still aware of the aliens but not uncomfortably so.

"You—you don't feel anything?"

He started. "How did you know I could feel things?"

"I didn't!" Ileth's hazel-green eyes were enormous. "Good Lord, Jon, I only thought you could sense their thoughts, maybe, if anything was around. I didn't... Can you feel things? You can, can't you? I should have guessed it."

Saxon's expression had grown grimmer with each word. When Ileth asked, "What are you?" in a hushed voice, he snapped.

"Homo Superior!"

"Homo Superior?" She looked startled, then raised her eyebrows. "You don't fancy yourself much, do you?"

They had drawn gradually away from the others. He looked back. Basil, the geographer, and his helper had set up their instruments. They were taking readings, making swift notations. They had the three dimensional camera recording impressions, and the automatic mapper was beginning to scratch a few tentative lines on its plastic rolls.

"I think we ought to stick together," Saxon volunteered. "I know it'll be impossible to keep the geographers by us, but the rest had better hang together."

Ileth shivered and asked, "Then there is something here?"

The silence was absolute. Not a breath of air stirred anywhere. Saxon hesitated, said at last, "Yes, I think so."

"What?"

"I don't know."

Clo-Javel approached them, straightening her short kilt-like skirts. The archaeologist's costume was brief and practical, but of more importance to Clo-Javel's way of thinking, the red skirt disclosed a goodly length of her really remarkable legs. Clo-Javel was even more proud of her legs than of her reconstruction of the New York skyscrapers. She said, "Did you ever see such buildings? What makes them look so weird?"

Saxon wrinkled his brow, his eyes returning to the glittering facade of cliff-like structures as they waited for the rest of their party to come up.

"I think," he said hesitantly, "it's because, it's because everything looks so new. As if the city was only finished yesterday and had never been used."

"That's it," Ileth burst out.

Mercedes joined them. She too, was wearing kilts, but hers were longer than Clo-Javel's and gray and her jacket was a commodious affair with many pockets. "What's that?" she asked catching the tail end of the conversation.

"The city looks as if it has never been lived in," Ileth explained.

Mercedes lit a cigarette, said, "Nonsense, whoever heard of building a city and then not using it."

"No." Clo-Javel agreed with the gray haired Mercedes. "It's not that altogether. Possibly it's built of some material impervious to decay. Saxon's a physicist." She gave him a brilliant smile. "He would know more about that than I do."

Clo-Javel pursed red lips. "It—it looks familiar."

There was a silence, then Mercedes said, "So it does. Though I can't put my finger on it. But that shouldn't be so strange. The creatures that built it might have been very similar to us. If I could lay my hands on some of their bones…" She laughed good humouredly. "I could tell you in a minute what they were like."

"Were?" Saxon thought, but he didn't express it aloud. He was conscious all the time of the presence of the aliens. It was like being in the midst of a crowded city street.

The semantics expert, the psycho-historian, and the ethnologist joined them in a body. They headed for the nearest building, a towering windowless structure of yellow crystal.

Saxon glanced back uneasily.

The helicopter stood silent and deserted in the center of the square. The geographer and his helper were disappearing down one of the canyon-like streets with their equipment.

"Look!" commanded Ileth pointing toward the face of the yellow structure. "Letters of some sort! There on the building. Maybe it's a sign."

They quickened their pace until they could describe the letters clearly.

Ileth gasped, "Oh!" and stopped uncertainly.

The rest of them came to a confused halt beside her, staring up at the sign in utter bewilderment. Saxon felt a chill creep up his spine. The sign read:

TIMES SQUARE

FOR as long as it takes to draw a startled breath there was silence; then they all began to babble at once. Clo-Javel made herself heard suddenly above the others. "I recognize it!" she cried in her ringing husky voice.

"What?"

"It's an exact reproduction of New York II! I knew the city looked familiar! I knew it!"

"New York II?" Saxon echoed. He was not strong in history and had only a faint recollection of a city by that name having once occupied the great Manhattan wastelands.

"Yes," Clo-Javel repeated. "It was the world capitol before Adirondaka was built. I had to study it when I was doing the reconstruction of New York I. There's a scale model of it in the Institute's museum. Isn't that right, Rufus?"

The psycho-historian nodded in a bemused fashion.

"Yes," he agreed. "New York II was built over the ruins of New York I which had been destroyed by the first atomic war. The second atomic war completely annihilated New York II as well as all the other big cities on Earth. Cities weren't built after that for almost five hundred years. Not until the Empire, in fact." He paused uncertainly. "I don't understand this."

Ileth asked, "You mean that this city is an exact reproduction of New York II, Clo?"

The woman nodded, her black eyes curiously frightened. "This is the amusement center. The yellow building housed the Tri-World Theatre."

"But I don't understand..." Ileth gazed helplessly at Saxon. "What is a reproduction of New York II doing here on a planet in the Alpha Centaurian system? We're over four light years from Sol. No one's ever been here before."

Saxon was conscious of bewilderment and fear muddling the girl's thoughts. His own mind couldn't quite grasp the fact that here was an exact replica of a Terran city. It was inexplicable. It didn't make sense. And, more than that, it was impossible!

He could read the same thoughts struggling against the fact in the minds of the others. He said, "Let's see what the buildings are like inside."

"Yes," agreed Ileth. She had edged close to Saxon. "Maybe we can find the answer inside."

They started for the impressive entrance of the Tri-World Theatre, halted again in near panic as the doors swung wide.

Ileth gasped, clutched at Saxon's arm, hanging onto it in desperation.

Before any of them could say anything, a voice blared forth. "...a thousand Ganymedian natives in the primitive ritualistic orgy of that weird little satellite. Hamura in the mating dance of the Ganymedians. Seats: three hundred and seventy-five dollars."

Clo-Javel's voice had lost its rich huskiness. It was a frightened quaver when she said, "It's a working model. Automatic, don't you see?" She giggled nervously, and paused.

"But the voice?" protested Ileth.

"Advertising," explained the archaeologist. "It's a mechanical voice, like the doors."

"Well, I'm not sure how much a dollar was," said Mercedes, "but three hundred and seventy-five for a seat seems rather exorbitant."

Rufus, the psycho-historian, was pale as a corpse. He swallowed, managed to splutter, "Inflation that followed the first atomic war. Inflation..." His voice trailed off as he stared beyond the gaping doors into the foyer of the empty theatre.

"Well, I'm not going in that place!" said the ethnologist suddenly. He was a goat-bearded little dandy. It was his first speech in some time.

Rufus, the psycho-historian, said, "I don't think I care to either."

"Nonsense!" exploded Mercedes. "There isn't anything in there. You can see for yourself. I'm going in."

"I think we should explore the city a bit further," Rufus protested. He glanced uneasily toward the helicopter. Basil and his helper were nowhere in sight.

Mercedes said, "Humph," gave her plump shoulders a shake and disappeared with short sturdy steps through the door.

"She shouldn't go in there alone," said Saxon starting after her. Ileth clung to his arm. "I'm coming along." They left the others standing huddled outside, watching them nervously.

THE foyer was carpeted ankle deep in mauve. Life-like, three-dimensional photographs of actors and actresses in every conceivable costume from none at all to the cumbersome furs of Titan lined the walls.

The magnificent foyer gave the startling impression that just the moment before, crowds of theatergoers had been surging across it. Saxon could feel the hair lift on the back of his neck.

"Where's Mercedes?" asked Ileth in a small voice.

Saxon glanced around, realized that the anthropologist wasn't in the foyer. "She must have gone into the theatre." He lifted his voice, called, "Mercedes. Mercedes!"

His voice echoed hollowly. There was no answer. Saxon and Ileth exchanged worried glances.

"Our voices probably don't carry beyond the foyer," Saxon reassured the girl. "The ancients were clever with sound."

They crossed the floor, their steps cushioned noiselessly in the thick mauve carpet. They went through the doors, past the automatic ticket taker and paused.

A vast amphitheater with curving rows of empty seats fell away below them like the terribly ancient Roman theatre at Pompeii. The walls by some trick of construction trapped the light, shedding it softly over the seats, concentrating it in a glowing pillar of illumination on the stage.

Suddenly, Ileth brought her hand to her mouth, a look of horror springing into her features. "Oh, my Lord!" she whispered. "Look!" and pointed at the floor at their feet. Saxon glanced down, caught his breath.

A puddle of clothes lay on the floor as if the middle aged, gray-haired anthropologist had just stepped out of them.

Saxon dropped to his knees beside the garments, turned them over. Sturdy leather walking shoes and heavy gray socks. Gray skirt and jacket. A stout brassiere and practical mannish shorts. They were so typically Mercedes, that Saxon felt a lump in his throat.

The socks were still in the shoes, brassiere inside the jacket. He stood up, feeling his palms begin to sweat. It was as if Mercedes had been suddenly dissipated into thin air, her clothes falling in on themselves.

He heard Ileth give a dry sob, realized suddenly that he felt no alien presence. He and the girl were alone in the theatre, alone as they'd been in the street that night in Adirondaka.

Saxon clenched his fist. "Let's get out of here. Quick!"

"But Mercedes?"

"She's gone! We can't help Mercedes now. The others! Hurry!"

They ran through the doorway back across the carpeted foyer, halting at the street.

Four little mounds of clothes met their eyes.

Saxon could feel his stomach knot inside himself. He felt the clothes. They were still warm from contact with the men's bodies. He stirred the brief red kilt that Clo-Javel had been wearing, saw with a macabre flash of humor that where Mercedes' underthings had been eminently practical, Clo-Javel didn't wear any at all.

Ileth suppressed a scream. "The helicopter! Look! It's gone, too!" Saxon glanced up in consternation.

The square was empty. The twin suns riding high in the sky beat down on bare plastic blocks where the helicopter had stood.

"We're hiking back to the ship—*now!*" Saxon said to the frightened girl.

"But it's twenty-five kilometers."

"So it's twenty-five kilometers. We can average four an hour or better. That's six hours. How many more hours of daylight have we?"

Ileth bit her lip, studied her chronometer.

"The days are short. The planet rotates in a little over fourteen hours. Alpha Centauri A sets first, in about an hour, I think. Then Alpha Centauri B about three hours later. Proxima rises about ten minutes after that but it doesn't cast much light."

"Never mind," he said almost roughly. "Come on. We'd better find the geographers quick."

THEY DID, a few minutes later, in one of the side canyons. That is, they found implements and two small piles of clothes. "I was afraid of this," said Saxon, his heart slowly sinking into his boots.

Ileth began to cry half in fright, half hysterically.

"None of that!" He shook her shoulders, until she stopped with a hiccup. Turning her loose, he bent over the instruments, secured a compass.

"We're northeast of the ship," he said. "that means if we travel in a southwesterly direction, we should hit it square on the nose. Let's hike!"

But they found it impossible to keep a true southwesterly course through the city. They walked along the deserted, resounding streets, their eyes filled with the fantastically lovely architecture of New York II, the flowing lines and gleaming planes of apartment houses built of a thousand substances from crystal to somber-veined black marble.

"To think," said Saxon, "that people, any people, could have found it in their hearts to destroy a work like this."

"I'm glad I've seen it," Ileth replied queerly, "even if I did have to come to Alpha Centauri. It's lovely." She shivered.

Saxon said in perplexity, "Why did they let us escape? I don't understand it."

"We were in the foyer, alone, when it—it must have happened," she suggested. "Maybe they overlooked us."

"Maybe," agreed Saxon doubtfully and paused.

They had come to the end of the city, which stopped abruptly as if it had been set down in the middle of the green rolling prairie. Beyond the last building, a herd of cannibal plants rolled by, browsing as they went.

"It's going to be damned tricky keeping a straight course across this," he said. "There doesn't seem to be a tree on the planet." He sighted the compass, picked out a round hill like the dome of a building, to the southwest. "We'll keep a little to the left of that hill."

ALPHA Centauri A was setting. By the time they had advanced a kilometer across the prairie it was gone. The orange light of Alpha Centauri B lent a queer unearthly complexion to the scene. It became perceptibly cooler, and a breeze sprang up from the east, bringing the faint scent of bitter almonds.

Saxon lengthened his stride. "We're not keeping to schedule," he said; then, "Look at that!"

A fawn colored creature like a large cat but with four pairs of legs, broke from a draw and went undulating across the grass.

"I'm getting tired," said Ileth in a small voice.

He took his eyes from the strange animal, studied the girl. The emotional turmoil, which they'd been through, had drained her of strength. Her features were white, drawn, her lids drooping over her hazel-green eyes. Her lashes, he thought, were the thickest curliest lashes he'd ever seen and red as her lustrous hair. He felt a tenderness well up inside him and banished it.

"We've got to make the ship. Walk until you drop. Then I'll carry you. But we have to get back as soon as possible."

Her features stiffened at the harshness of his words. He caught a weary flash of anger in her thoughts, then she turned and began to plod again toward the southwest.

"Faster," said Saxon.

Alpha Centauri B was setting when they reached the domed hill, which Saxon had lined up with the compass. He left Ileth stretched exhausted at the base and climbed to the summit. His eyes swept the horizons with the last orange rays of the sun, but the *Shooting Star* was still not in sight.

By the time he rejoined Ileth, it was dark. "Did you see it?" the girl asked in a sleepy voice.

"No. We haven't come far enough, I suppose. We'll have to wait until Proxima rises before we can go on. That'll give us a chance to rest. How long before Proxima comes up?"

"Ten or fifteen minutes." She hesitated. "I'm cold."

Saxon put his arms around the shivering girl, pulled her against him. She gave a little sigh, laid her head on his shoulder. He caught her sleepy thoughts, *"Two times two is four. Three times two is six,"* and chuckled to himself.

The darkness was not dispelled very much when Proxima rose above the hills like a sullen red-hot drop of metal. The light was red and wavering like the shimmering heat waves above a brush fire. Saxon could not see very well or very far. Nevertheless he wakened Ileth.

She rubbed her eyes, glanced about her in consternation. The change in light had brought about a startling change in the scenery. It looked as if it were bathed in blood.

She said, "Oh, Jon, I wish we were home. I wish we'd never come on this horrible expedition."

He didn't look up from his compass. "The ship can't be much further." He spotted the black gash of a gully a hundred yards ahead. "We'll walk to the gully, then pick out another object."

"I'm still tired. I don't feel as if I'd slept at all."

"You didn't—much. Only about ten minutes. Come on."

They reached the gully and Saxon found a cone-shaped hill looming up redly almost a quarter of a mile further on. They set out for it, Ileth holding his hand.

Their progress was necessarily slower because Saxon had to stop often and consult the compass. Even so, he began to be afraid that they had overshot the ship in the dark.

Slowly Proxima Centauri blazed its blood red path across the night sky.

Not far from Proxima a star twinkled faintly, steadily. It was about in the position that Sol should be. He wondered if it was.

"It's growing lighter," said Ileth.

Saxon glanced toward the east, recognized the graying darkness that heralded the dawn. He said, "Alpha Centauri A's rising. Maybe we can see where we are."

The light was quickening fast with dawn. Saxon climbed to the crest of a ridge, stared off into the southwest.

All at once his heart stood still. He called, "Ileth! Ileth! Come up here!"

The girl ran up the ridge, the urgency in his voice dispelling her weariness. "What is it, Jon?"

He pointed ahead. "Aren't those the hills south of the ship?"

She narrowed her eyes, studying the blue outlines in the dawn light. "Yes. But, Jon, where is the ship?"

He pointed at a blackened circle in the grass not an eighth of a kilometer distant. The circle was almost a thousand yards in diameter.

"That's where our jets burned the grass when we landed. That's where the *Shooting Star* was yesterday!"

In ten minutes they were tramping back and forth across the blackened circle of grass, kicking up little puffs of ashes. The mark of the jets were there, pressed deep in the soft soil. But those and the charred vegetation were the only signs that a ship had ever rested there.

Ileth flung herself dejectedly to the grass at the edge of the circle. "I'm so hungry and bone weary and thirsty and disappointed, I could cry."

Saxon sat down beside her. "I don't understand it," he said for the hundredth time. "I don't understand any of it."

All at once, his scalp began to prickle its warning and Saxon recognized the alien feel. At the same instant Ileth screamed, leaping to her feet. Saxon felt his mouth go dry, his stomach contract as he stumbled erect beside her.

Not ten yards distant, in the path of the rising sun, a naked man was materializing before their eyes. Saxon could see the grass and the hills and a segment of Alpha Centauri A through the man's body.

A thought struck into Saxon's mind. *"So there you are."* It emanated from the Alien. *"We were afraid you might have gotten clean away."*

Saxon realized the man was quite solid now, standing with bare feet planted in the pale green grass. There was an instrument like a watch strapped to his wrist. He was holding a small shiny cylinder.

Saxon caught an echo of Ileth's thought. *"Oh. Lord, he's naked as a grape!"*

The man leveled the cylinder. There was a brief flash.

Saxon felt an instant's giddiness, a rapid dissolution, then nothing.

CHAPTER EIGHT

JON SAXON COULDN'T HAVE been unconscious but a fraction of a second because he didn't have time to fall. He came to himself swaying dizzily, nauseated as if with space sickness.

He opened his eyes. He was blind!

The shock left him numb. Then gradually, like a flower unfolding its petals to the light, he felt his extra-human sixth sense assume control.

He became aware of the grass and the sun and the distant hills. Everything registered in varying degrees of grayness. It wasn't grayness exactly, but the word came as near to describing the peculiar impressions that external objects were registering on his sixth sense as his vocabulary could supply.

He didn't picture his environment; he realized it. The burned circle of grass, the naked alien...

A second shock rocked Saxon to his heels. The Alien!

Tentatively, almost timidly, he examined the strange figure confronting him. The man, for man he appeared to be, stood quietly several paces away, sizing up Saxon with an equal degree of caution. The analogy to two strange dogs eyeing each other belligerently, but each afraid to make the first move, was so ludicrous that Saxon chuckled although no sound issued from his lips.

He sensed his opponent relax. The fellow was big the way Saxon was big, and the same virility radiated from him like a physical force.

The impressions received via his sixth sense were gaining in vividness. Saxon had never fully appreciated its scope before.

Then with the force of a blow, Ileth's terrified thoughts penetrated sharply to his mind.

"I must be dead! Oh God, I'm dead!"

Saxon could perceive the girl cowering above a small pile of clothes, frightened, helpless, blind. She didn't have his extra-human sixth sense to substitute for sight. She was trembling violently, a slim-naked wraith without substance.

The little pile of clothes at her feet made it suddenly clear what had befallen Mercedes and the crew, what had happened to Ileth and himself. In some fashion, the Aliens had transmuted them into a space where their three dimensional organs of perception no longer registered.

He moved to the girl, touched her arm.

Saxon was not conscious of a sense of contact, but a vague shock like a weak electric current ran up his arm to his brain. Ileth flinched back in terror.

Again he touched her arm, thinking, *"Ileth, am I getting through? Ileth, am I getting through?"* over and over again.

"Yes," came the unexpected answer. *"Yes. Yes. Is it you, Jon? We're dead, you know, Jon."*

"No," he thought. *"We're not dead. We've been transmuted but we're not dead."*

A command rang sharply in his disembodied mind. *"Lead the girl and follow me!"*

Saxon's attention swung back to the Alien, perceived the man threatening him with the cylinder, which had blasted them into this indeterminate dimension.

"Suppose I refuse?" he thought.

"I'm afraid that you underestimate the range of effect of this weapon." The Alien brandished the cylinder again. *"Follow me."*

Saxon capitulated, touched Ileth. *"Keep in contact with me. I'll guide you."* He began to move after the stranger who was already at a distance.

He didn't know how long they walked. Time had no expression in this state. Alpha Centauri A hung always in the same spot just above the horizon. He thought of Villainowski's inverted formula— "To travel through time during a passage of space." The Little Death must be like this, if one were conscious.

He was still turning it over in his mind when he perceived the station.

The station appeared to be a cubical structure like a large plastic block, except that the matter of which it was formed wasn't matter at all. It was energy, Saxon sensed, pulsating sheets of energy that must not be visible in the normal, three-dimensional world.

The Alien stood to one side, motioned them through the shimmering walls.

Saxon was conscious of a throbbing rhythm, which swept through him like the hum of a dynamo. He experienced the eerie giddiness for the second time and groped for Ileth before he blanked out.

THIS time Saxon was longer regaining consciousness. He came out from under the effects of the pulsation, feeling his flesh solid again. Air warmed and caressed his skin. He was materialized, he saw, as he leaped to his feet and opened his eyes.

He felt vaguely overwhelmed by the return of his senses. He had never before appreciated their infinite variety. The walls were yellow, lemon yellow; the floor cool and firm underfoot; the air had a faint odor of bitter almonds; and Ileth...

He said, "Open your eyes, Ileth. You'll be able to see better that way."

The girl's eyes popped open. She took one look at Saxon, then at herself. Her eyes grew rounder, her throat flamed.

She gasped, "Oh! You should have let me keep my eyes shut," and whipped her back to him.

She must have realized instantly that the view she presented was no better screened, for she sat down with a thump, saying, "Oh!" again. Then, in an embarrassed voice, "This is just like a dream I had once. Only everyone but me wore clothes in the dream, and there isn't a fig leaf between the three of us."

"The three of us?"

Saxon glanced around, discovered the Alien rummaging in one of the cabinets, from which he produced three of the gleaming kilts, tossed them each one.

"You humans," he said in an amused tone and perfect English, "have odd notions about concealing yourselves. Here."

Saxon gratefully buckled his kilt in place, examined the material. The threads were almost weightless and glowed like strands of light. With a start, he recalled where he had seen them before.

The man and the woman had been wearing kilts like these in his vision during the Little Death. Then...

His mind refused to entertain the possibility. And yet it was a piece of everything else. His inability to remember his childhood. The development of first a sixth sense at twenty-seven, then a seventh at thirty-one.

He strode abruptly to the windows and looked out.

The windows were at an elevation and gave a view of the strangest city he had ever beheld.

There were houses, at least they could be houses, spaced entirely without relation to each other and surrounded by immense park-like grounds. There were no congested areas within his range of vision. Neither was he able to discover roads or sidewalks, fences or walls anywhere.

Alpha Centauri A was still just rising, its orange twin not yet above the hills, which he could see in the distance.

He turned wonderingly back into the room.

Their guard regarded them in amusement. "Sit down," he suggested, indicating a bench.

They seated themselves.

"Ask him what they're going to do with us, Jon." Ileth nudged Saxon in the ribs.

Saxon cleared his throat.

Before he could speak, the guard smiled and said, "I haven't the faintest idea how they plan to dispose of you. Even if I did, that would be for Them to tell you." He nodded toward a closed door on their right. "They'll send for you any moment now."

"Who are 'they'?" Saxon asked.

"The Elders."

"What planet is this?"

"Vark." The guard's voice was pleasant. He smiled faintly when he talked. "The fourth planet of the sun you call Alpha Centauri A. This is the city of Ghibellena." He nodded out the windows.

"How did we get here? Teleportation?"

"Not exactly."

There was a momentary silence while the Alien observed them with that amused gleam in his eye. Then Saxon tried again. "Who are you? Why have you captured us?"

The man nodded briefly again towards the closed door. "You'll learn that in there—if They see fit to tell you."

"Where are the rest of the crew? Dead? In prison?"

"Oh, no. They've been taken to Zara."

"Zara? Where's Zara?"

"Zara is a satellite of the third planet. The one we call Tunis."

"What is that city we saw? The deserted one near the ship?"

Again the man smiled and nodded toward the door. "If They see fit to tell you."

Saxon shrugged burly shoulders. "How do you make yourselves invisible?"

Surprisingly enough the man answered.

"It's a refinement of your stellar drive, an excursion into the time field. In fact, it was discovered almost a hundred of your years ago by a Terran. A Dr. Walter."

Saxon looked disconcerted. Ileth swallowed, her eyes as round as saucers. Suddenly her hand squeezed his arm.

"The door! It's opening!"

"You may go in," said their guard. "They're ready for you."

Saxon had risen uncertainly. He looked at the door, which was receding into the wall. Through the portal, he glimpsed a terrace or a balcony, roofless. Beyond and below the terrace was a yellow sea stretching to the horizon, its cadmium waves frothing against a beach of black sand.

"They're expecting you," the guard prompted.

Saxon shrugged. Taking Ileth's arm, he went through the opening. The door slid shut behind them.

THE BALCONY, Saxon saw, was paved checkerboard fashion with green and yellow blocks. At the left, out of sight from the entrance, was a twenty-foot table of pale green stone. Seven incredibly old men sat behind the table.

No one said anything.

Saxon took the initiative, advanced to within six feet of the pale green table. His dark gray eyes narrowed. He was vaguely conscious of a flow of thought passing among the seven old men like conversation, but its content escaped him. His jaw jutted angrily.

"Control your anger, my son," said the old man in the center. "Your thoughts should be respectful in the presence of your elders."

Saxon concealed his astonishment, asking, "Might I inquire what this mummery is all about?" He became aware again of the hidden thoughts flowing between them.

Then the old man in the center said, "I am the moderator, my son. Your mind, we have perceived, teems with questions. We have decided that from the psychological angle, certain of these questions can now be answered."

"Psychological angle?" Saxon felt confused. The deviousness of the Aliens, the maddening superiority, which they assumed, began to get under his skin. With an effort, he got a grip on himself, returned their curious stares.

The seven old men were wrinkled, emaciated. Once they had been big men like Saxon, but the years had wasted their flesh.

"That's better," approved the Moderator, referring to Saxon's change of tactics. "Now for your questions," and he seemed to look straight into Saxon's mind.

"Very early in our history," began the Moderator after a moment, "we learned that we advanced in the physical sciences by trial and error. A disheartening process, because only so many combinations can be tried in a single lifetime..."

"What the hell has this got to do with us?" Saxon interrupted harshly.

"Patience, my son. I'm explaining the relation between our world and the third planet of Sol which you call Earth."

A little muscle began to jump in Saxon's jaw.

"Trial and error," the old man began again. "A slow heartbreaking process, and one which in its nature is inescapable. At least, so we thought until quite recently." He paused, tugged at his lower lip with thumb and forefinger.

Saxon mastered an impulse to shout, "Get to the point!"

"Recently," went on the moderator, "we tried an experiment in our biological laboratories which we hoped would speed up the trial-and-error formula.

"By exposing the germ plasm of a semi-intelligent anthropoid inhabiting the fourth planet of this system to hard radiations, we succeeded in creating a mutant, a biologic sport who's life span was only an instant of time. It matured, mated and died in an incredibly brief period.

"They were startlingly prolific as well; they multiplied like—like—" he groped for a simile— "like guinea pigs or rats.

"Furthermore, they early exhibited the most amazing ingenuity. In twenty generations they had fire; in thirty, crude implement of stone."

Saxon, unable to restrain his impatience longer cried, "The point, man—get to the point."

The old man gave Saxon a steely look. "We recognized," he went on stiffly, "the significance of our mutation. As soon as the semi-intelligent sports developed a science, we could expect the trial and error method to be speeded up. A lifetime of experiment to them was only a moment to us.

"We isolated them on the fifth planet of our sun. But it soon became apparent that they constituted a dangerous menace even that close. They were so fecund, and their ferocity was appalling. Wars broke out between various tribes. They murdered each other by the thousands."

Gradually Saxon's interest had been caught by the history of the semi-reasoning mutants whose ferocity and proliferation had constituted a menace to their creators. He glanced at Ileth, discovered her spellbound.

The Moderator's voice was growing thinner.

"Luckily," he was saying, "stellar travel was accomplished at this time. We exported several thousand of the creatures to another star system and destroyed the rest.

"The environment on the planet where we transplanted our colony of humanoids was ideal for our purpose—harsh and savage. Several species of bipeds with rudimentary intelligence already inhabited the planet, but our own culture speedily wiped them out and were happily warring among themselves..."

A suspicion began to grow in Saxon's mind. He blurted, "On what planet did you introduce this culture?"

The Moderator paused, stared Saxon coolly in the eye.

"Earth!" he said.

SAXON and Ileth looked at each other incredulously, unable to comprehend the significance of the Moderator's answer.

"Earth?" repeated Saxon. "I don't understand."

The Moderator wrinkled his brow, and said, "I don't know how to put it any more clearly. We transplanted our biological sports to Earth. The two sub-human races which our humanoids exterminated were the Cro-Magnards and the Neanderthalers."

Saxon's brain reeled, "Do you mean that man as we know him, homo sapiens, originated in your laboratories as—as an experiment?"

He heard Ileth laugh hysterically.

"Precisely," replied the Moderator. "And I might add that the experiment has proven successful. During the last thousand years they have supplied us with hundreds of discoveries and developments. The real nature of the space time continuum, for example.

"The creatures are inordinately clever at the physical sciences—as was to be expected from an emotionally unstable, rationalizing mammal under the pressure of such an antagonistic environment. Our own laboratories have become, for all practical purposes, unnecessary!"

Ileth was staring at the Moderator with wide horrified eyes. "I," she gasped. "I am a humanoid? I don't live but a moment? I'm prolific and savage and—and clever like a monkey? Why, you shriveled up old bag of bones, that's the most stupid pack of lies I've ever heard!"

The Moderator regarded her compassionately. "You haven't changed because I've told you the truth. Your life expectation is no shorter. It's a matter of relativity. To us our ten thousand years seems no longer than your three score and ten does to you."

"Ten thousand years?" exploded Saxon. The sum was so staggering that it was only a figure to him. "Then—" he began, but the Moderator answered before he could speak.

"No. I was not born when the experiment with the humanoids began. They were developed some twenty-five thousand years ago."

Ileth began to laugh crazily, unable to stop. In a moment she would be hysterical. Saxon shook her roughly. "Stop it!"

"I—I—I can't," she giggled. "Either he's mad or I am." Her words ended in a flood of tears.

Saxon put his arm around the girl, turned back to the Moderator. "It was done with hard radiations?"

"Yes. In the resultant mutants their metabolism had been accelerated beyond our wildest expectation. Their life cycle geared to their metabolism passed through its different phases like—like..." again he fished in Saxon's mind for a simile. "Like a meteor. By artificially slowing down their metabolism they returned to their normal life span.

"You've been very curious about the replica of New York II which you saw when you landed."

Saxon nodded, trying to conceal a thought, which had begun to take shape in the back of his mind.

"It's just that. A replica of a city built during the Atomic Age by the humanoids. Their constant implacable wars are so savage that we've found it necessary to duplicate their work here, if we hope to preserve any of it for study."

Saxon narrowed his eyes, asked, "You spoke of the menace of having such savage neighbors. Just how serious was such a threat?"

THE Moderator smiled and glanced at his constituents. Saxon strained to grasp the thoughts flowing between them, but failed utterly.

"Admirable!" the Moderator commented suddenly. "Your reactions, my son, are leading us to hope we may turn in the most optimistic report."

Saxon stared at him as if he were crazy. Ileth's tears had subsided to a sniffle.

"Now for your question," said the Moderator and coughed again.

"The menace was real, not imaginary. We had created a monster that would be either a marvelous scientific instrument, or—the means of our destruction.

"Remember, my son, time is relative. These creatures lived, fought, loved, begat children, carried on scientific research and died, all in seventy short years. They existed at fever intensity. Their metabolism burns them up.

"Our lives are adjusted to a span of ten thousand years. We have a total population of little over a million. We are neither a war-like people, nor a highly industrialized people.

"In one of their generations the humanoids accomplish almost as much as we do in one of ours. Think, my son, they perform in seventy years what it takes us ten thousand to do.

"If it ever came to hostilities between us we'd be doomed, overwhelmed almost before we realized what was happening."

Saxon listened in astonishment. The thought in the back of his mind kept trying to push to the fore, but he repressed it, afraid that the Aliens might see it.

"Their amazing fecundity," the Moderator was saying, "their short life spans, their ingenuity and ferocity made them a very real menace even isolated outside our stellar system. Fortunately, we also foresaw the inevitable crisis and prepared for it."

"Crisis?" Saxon echoed.

"The time when the humanoids would reach our scientific level and surpass us," said the Moderator in a grim voice. "That time has arrived!"

CHAPTER NINE

SOMEWHERE A BELL BEGAN TO ring shrilly. Saxon saw an expression of annoyance pass across the Moderator's wrinkled visage. He pressed a button set in the tabletop. The bell stopped ringing. A voice began to speak in an alien tongue directly behind Saxon. The burly nuclear physicist spun around in surprise.

He was looking into the control room of a small private space yacht!

The deception was so realistic that Saxon gasped before he noticed the three beams of light converging from lenses in the wall, focusing at a point directly behind him to form the solid appearing image. A three dimensional televisor complete with sound!

Then all speculation was driven from his mind as he recognized the figure who was speaking.

Mustapha IX, Supreme Autocrat of the Terran Empire!

The image of Mustapha sat stiffly in an acceleration chair before the control panel of the space yacht. His voice, rattling away in the strange language, was high, tense, frightened.

Saxon, unable to understand, looked over his shoulder at the seven old men. They were all on their feet, staring in disbelief at the three dimensional image. The Moderator's hands began to tremble. He sat down as if his knees had turned to water.

The voice rattled on and on.

At last Mustapha IX quit talking. The Moderator pressed the button. The image dissolved.

A stunned silence followed, as one by one the old men sank back to their seats. Saxon, devoured with curiosity, asked, "What was it?"

The Moderator gave him a level glance. "That was the man you know as Mustapha IX, Supreme Autocrat of the Terran Empire. He was reporting from his private yacht, which has just emerged from the time field and is decelerating. It'll be a week before he lands on Vark."

"Mustapha IX?" Saxon burst out. "Here on Vark? But that's impossible. What's he doing—"

"There's been civil war," the Moderator interrupted savagely. "General Atomic has overthrown Government. General Atomic is the Terran Government now!"

"But I don't see..." protested Saxon.

"Bah! I spoke of controls. Naturally our first necessity has been to control the humanoid's government. The Supreme Autocrats have all been Varkans, our governors, which we sent to Earth!

"Now Mustapha IX has had to flee for his life. Most of our agents on Earth have been murdered. Only a handful escaped with him!"

The Moderator pressed another button, began to speak rapidly, tonelessly in the alien language into a microphone. The thoughts of the seven old men were flashing back and forth like streaks of light behind their mental barrier. The crisis, Saxon realized, had arrived with a vengeance!

Suddenly the guard came running through the door in answer to a summons by the Moderator. For the first time Saxon intercepted a thought as the Moderator directed the guard to take the prisoners away.

"Send the girl to Zara," he commanded the guard. *"Confine the man here until we can check results!"*

"Come along," said the guard in a tight voice to Saxon and Ileth. He took hold of Ileth's arm. The girl shrank away from him, frightened by the swift and ominous change, which had come over their captors.

Saxon's eyes went bleak. The guard jerked back as he caught a glimpse of Saxon's intentions, but he wasn't quick enough.

Saxon's balled fist caught him on his left cheekbone, sent him sprawling to the checkered pavement. Saxon was on him like a wolf. Wrenching the cylinder from the stunned guard's belt, he backed off swinging the unfamiliar weapon in a menacing arc.

He saw the withered faces of the Elders blanch. They pressed stiffly against the back of their chairs, jaws sagging. The guard scrambled to his feet. He shook his head groggily but made no move to attack Saxon.

Triumph welled up inside Jon Saxon. He said, "The shoe's on the other foot. I don't know how this damned thing works, but there's a button. Unless you start answering my questions straight we'll see what happens if I press it."

He paused. The seven old men glared at him but said nothing.

"How did General Atomic discover your agents? Why didn't their invisibility protect them?"

The Moderator moistened his lips. "The humanoids devised a machine that detects us. An adaption of the thought projector, which enabled them to detect our telepathic potential. Once they could isolate our thought waves, they were able to trace them to their source by a process similar to locating the source of a radio beam."

Saxon narrowed his eyes, recalling the thought projector, which the radiation branch of Government's Bureau of Research had been experimenting with. So that's how General Atomic had uncovered the Aliens.

"General Atomic," the Moderator was saying, "suspected the existence of mutants, telepaths, ever since an agent of theirs by the name of Emil turned in a report on you!"

Saxon started.

The Moderator's first fright was over, he realized. The old man was regarding him with a faint smile.

Saxon glanced behind him in alarm; but there was nothing there. He clenched his fist until the knuckles whitened. "What other methods did you use to keep the humanoids in check?"

There was a subtle change in the voice of the Moderator when he answered. It was ringing, hard. "As I said, we foresaw this crisis. To discourage stellar travel we planted a pathologic fear of deep space in the humanoid subconscious.

"Certain of their discoveries we have suppressed. Notably, the space-time stellar drive. The Little Death, as you call it, has been discovered three separate times in the past thousand years."

"What?"

"Yes. Are you surprised? Once by an unknown scientist, once by a physicist, Dr. Walter, and lastly by Dr. Villainowski."

Although Saxon still held the alien weapon, he had the uncomfortable sensation that a trap had been sprung and the Moderator was only waiting for it to close on him.

With a suffocating tenseness, he asked, "What am I?"

"You," said the Moderator, "are a test experiment!"

"What?"

"A test experiment. Your psychological reactions will depend the ultimate fate of the humanoids!"

"A test experiment," he repeated dazedly. "What do you mean?"

"Simply this. For some time we've realized that steps must be taken to curb the rapaciousness of the humanoids."

"But me…"

The Moderator held up his hand.

"I'm coming to you. If the ruthless savagery of the humanoids was instinctive, part of their heredity, there was little that could be done except destroy them.

"But if, on the other hand, their natures resulted from the pressure of their environment, we might be able to modify that environment and salvage our experiment."

"But what the hell am I? What did you mean when you said I was a test experiment?"

The Moderator seemed to have forgotten the existence of Saxon's weapon. He tugged at his lower lip with thumb and forefinger. "You are not a humanoid. You are one of us, a Varkan. We placed you as a baby on Earth to be raised as a humanoid."

"I was eleven," protested Saxon.

"A mere baby still, with psychological plasticity." The Moderator waved the objection aside. "If your disposition hardened into humanoid characteristics, then we would be safe in assuming that the humanoids, too, were a product of their environment.

"Of course, there were factors we couldn't control. The natural unfolding of your sixth and seventh senses in early childhood—"

Saxon burst out, "But I was twenty-seven when I developed a sixth sense and thirty-one—"

"My son, that's quite true. But you're only in your adolescence now."

"At thirty-eight," said Saxon in disbelief, "I'm an adolescent?"

The Moderator nodded. "And precocious at that!"

Ileth giggled again nervously.

SAXON gave a short laugh. He had a feeling that he had been stuffed too full of information. He couldn't digest it. In spite of the suspicions he had entertained concerning his birth, he was unable to really believe that he was an Alien!

He glanced suddenly at Ileth. The girl had shrunk away from him as if he were a leper. Her hazel-green eyes were horrified. All at once, she began to cry.

Saxon tried to pat her shoulder, but she wrenched away. The action drove a needle of pain into his heart. He realized in a numbed fashion how fond he had grown of the girl.

"Fond, hell!" he thought savagely. "I'm in love with her."

"My son," came the hated voice of the Moderator, "she is not for you."

"What do you mean?" Saxon shouted.

The Moderator regarded him a moment, his eyes veiled. Then, "The psychologist is ready to give you his report. As a true human, you have the right to hear it."

A shriveled, wrinkled man at the end of the table began to address Saxon in a dry voice.

"I've been probing your reactions as the truth was revealed to you. You can understand the importance of an accurate judgment, when you know that the fate of our experiment rests on the manner in which you conformed to a humanoid environment."

"Experiment be damned!" Saxon flung out. "What about me?"

The psychologist permitted himself a vague smile. "Your reactions have been typically humanoid.

"You have been bewildered, frightened, angry.

"You tried to think first of some way by which you could destroy us. Failing that, you cast about in your mind for some compromise which would cause us to hold our hand until we could be either conquered or wiped out—preferably wiped out. These are typically humanoid reactions to a dangerous foe.

"Under the circumstances we can preserve our experiment if we can modify the humanoids' environment."

Saxon felt relief. Whatever the Aliens planned, they weren't going to destroy mankind.

The psychologist having delivered his report, the Moderator resumed, "It is unfortunate in a way for you, my son, that the test has been so favorable to the humanoids.

"They live and die so fast that in a few generations we can correct their savage dispositions.

"But you have solidified in the humanoid mold. You will have to undergo a dangerous operation. Our psychologist must induce infantile retrogression in you. When you have been reduced mentally, to the age of eleven, then your re-education can begin.

"I'll be perfectly frank. You have about one chance in ten of retaining your sanity. The danger lies in that retrogression once activated in your brain cells—it cannot always be halted."

Saxon's laugh was a croak. "You forget I've still the weapon."

The Moderator said, "It's time that this nonsense stopped. We've allowed you to retain the cylinder in order to observe your reactions. Look around you!"

Saxon spun around.

Materializing like gray wraiths, a dozen figures were taking substance behind him. They were all armed with shining cylinders.

"Drop it!" commanded the Moderator.

Saxon's weapon clanged against the pavement.

ILETH suppressed a scream, swayed, half-fainting. Saxon caught her before she fell. The girl recovered, flung her arms about his neck.

"You can't do it!" she stormed at the Elders. "You can't. I love him. I don't care what he is, I love him, I tell you!"

"Take them away!" the Moderator said imperiously.

The wraiths had grown solid. They began to close in.

Saxon's spine stiffened. He said, "Wait a moment," in a breathless voice. "Have you overlooked the five sets of plans for Villainowski's stellar drive? The ones that were stolen from Government's Research Building?"

The Moderator's face went gray. For the second time Saxon intercepted a thought flowing between the seven old men.

A fear thought! Pure funk!

Saxon's heart leaped like an arrow as the realization burst on him that the seven old men were terrified of the humanoids. They were so badly frightened that for a moment their guard had relaxed and the fear thought had escaped past their mental barriers.

If only there was a way to exploit their fear. He felt hope surging back through his veins.

"Already," he shouted, "General Atomic must be manufacturing the ships. And you can't stop it. The secret of stellar travel is loose among the humanoids!"

"We know of the loss of the plans. General Atomic is laying the keels of thousands of the new-type ships. But that doesn't affect your fate in the least."

"Doesn't it?" said Saxon harshly. "I'm the only Varkan who can compete with the humanoids. I'm the only one who's been conditioned to the speed of their reflexes."

"You're a dangerous anti-social!" the Moderator snapped. "Your auto-reactions approach the humanoid level because you're still a child with a child's adaptiveness. When you mature you'll appreciate the difference. We wouldn't dare use you even if you could do anything. If worst comes to worst we can destroy our experiment!"

Saxon laughed at him. "And how many generations of humanoids would have passed away before you could wipe out a culture that's spread to all the planets of its solar system? Why, they'll be swarming over Vark from pole to pole before you can prepare to repel them."

The Moderator winced, tried to interrupt, but Saxon was inexorable.

"You might have been able to destroy them while you had them isolated in their own Solar System. But they're free now. Free to expand through the Galaxy!"

Saxon paused. The idea sprouting some time ago had begun to bear fruit. He pushed it resolutely out of his mind lest they intercept it.

The Moderator asked with narrowed eyes, "You have an idea, haven't you?"

Saxon could feel the Aliens probing at his thoughts like a scalpel laying bare his skull.

"Two times two is four. Three times two is six," he thought hastily and realized the seven old men were on the verge of apoplexy.

There was a tense moment of silence as their wills clashed. Then the Moderator asked, "What's your price?"

"Freedom for myself and the crew. Hands-off policy for the humanoids."

The silence deepened.

Again Saxon became aware of those flickering baffling thoughts as the seven old men conferred behind their mental shields.

At last, grudgingly, the Moderator spoke, "That depends on your success."

Saxon didn't relax. He had won only if he had guessed the right answer to a question that had been obsessing him. If he was right, he would need no guarantee to hold the Aliens to their promise.

"You said that when the metabolism of the humanoids was slowed they returned to their normal life span. Does that mean that you can actually lengthen their lives to equal yours?"

The Moderator looked puzzled, nodded. "A comparatively simple operation, but…"

"But nothing!" Saxon almost shouted. "If their life span is the same as yours, then they'll be on the same time scale. Their fecundity is the direct result of their shortened life cycle. They'll no longer constitute a menace!"

Hope blazed temporarily in the Moderator's eyes, then went out. When he spoke next his voice was cold, dead.

"But that takes time. Before we could effect the change several generations of humanoids would have lived and died. We'd be conquered!"

Saxon laughed outright. "Of course, you people couldn't effect the change quick enough, but other humanoids could. You have Ileth here. She's a General Atomic agent. You have the crew and some of the best brains on Earth isolated on Zara. They could do it!"

The Moderator drew in his breath sharply. "But would they be willing to cooperate?"

"What a question!" roared Saxon. "Would mankind be willing to increase their life span ten thousand years? They'll jump at it!"

ZARA was a diminutive green little world, held in thrall by the third planet of Alpha Centauri A. A miniature heaven of soft breezes and crystal streams and gravity so slight that Saxon felt buoyant as a bubble.

He said in rare good humor, "So there it is. The Varkans can't slow the metabolic rate of billions of humanoids by force or by themselves in time."

He was surrounded by the members of the expedition, to whom he had just explained the proposal of the Aliens to extend mankind's normal life span to an unthinkable age.

With his arm around Ileth's slim waist, he had watched suspicion give way to hope and hope to wild enthusiasm. Only Villainowski appeared disgruntled.

"It's more than I can stomach," growled the Chief, "to think of perpetuating General Atomic in power practically forever."

Saxon leaned close, said in a lowered voice, "You don't believe that if the people have ten thousand years to contemplate the iniquity of General Atomic, they'll continue to be duped. It'll be the death blow to all the big corporations."

He straightened, returning his arm to Ileth's waist. "There's no reason for you to return to Earth with the rest of them, Villainowski. There's a lot to see here, a lot to learn. Ileth and I are going to spend…"

He frowned, called, "Hey, Mercedes. You're the anthropologist. What was that barbaric custom practiced by newly-married couples during the pre-Atom age?"

"The honeymoon." Mercedes chuckled, turned to the faintly pink Ileth, pinched her cheek. "Don't look so frightened, child. The first ten thousand years are the hardest."

THE END

If you've enjoyed this book, you will not want to miss these terrific titles…

ARMCHAIR SCI-FI & HORROR DOUBLE NOVELS, $12.95 each

D-131 **COSMIC KILL** by Robert Silverberg
BEYOND THE END OF SPACE by John W. Campbell

D-132 **THE DARK OTHER** by Stanley Weinbaum)
WITCH OF THE DEMON SEAS by Poul Anderson

D-133 **PLANET OF THE SMALL MEN** by Murray Leinster
MASTERS OF SPACE by E. E. "Doc" Smith & E. Everett Evans

D-134 **BEFORE THE ASTEROIDS** by Harl Vincent
SIXTH GLACIER, THE by Marius

D-135 **AFTER WORLD'S END** by Jack Williamson
THE FLOATING ROBOT by David Wright O'Brien

D-136 **NINE WORLDS WEST** by Paul W. Fairman
FRONTIERS BEYOND THE SUN by Rog Phillips

D-137 **THE COSMIC KINGS** by Edmond Hamilton
LONE STAR PLANET by H. Beam Piper & John J. McGuire

D-138 **BEYOND THE DARKNESS** by S. J. Byrne
THE FIRELESS AGE by David H. Keller, M. D.

D-139 **FLAME JEWEL OF THE ANCIENTS** by Edwin L. Graber
THE PIRATE PLANET by Charles W. Diffin

D-140 **ADDRESS: CENTAURI** by F. L. Wallace
IF THESE BE GODS by Algis Budrys

ARMCHAIR SCIENCE FICTION CLASSICS, $12.95 each

C-58 **THE WITCHING NIGHT**
by Leslie Waller

C-59 **SEARCH THE SKY**
by Frederick Pohl and C. M. Kornbluth

C-60 **INTRIGUE ON THE UPPER LEVEL**
by Thomas Temple Hoyne

ARMCHAIR SCI-FI & HORROR GEMS SERIES, $12.95 each

G-15 **SCIENCE FICTION GEMS, Vol. Eight**
Keith Laumer and others

G-16 **HORROR GEMS, Vol. Eight**
Algernon Blackwood and others

If you've enjoyed this book, you will not want to miss these terrific titles…

ARMCHAIR SCI-FI & HORROR DOUBLE NOVELS, $12.95 each